John Adams

Architect of Freedom (1735-1826)

Joseph Cowley is the author of more than thirteen books, including an anthology *The Best of Joseph Cowley;* the novels *The Chrysanthemum Garden, Home by Seven, Dust Be My Destiny, The House on Huntington Hill,* and *Landscape with Figures*; the story collections *The Night Billy Was Born and Other Love Stories,* and *Do You Like It and Other Stories;* the plays *The Stargazers, A Jury of His Peers,* and *Twin Bill* (*I Love You, I Love You* and *My Life with Women*); and *The Executive Strategist: An Armchair Guide to Scientific Decision-Making.*

John Adams

Architect of Freedom (1735-1826)

Joseph Cowley

iUniverse, Inc.

New York   Bloomington

iUniverse books may be ordered through booksellers or by contacting:

iUniverse
1663 Liberty Drive
Bloomington, IN 47403
www.iuniverse.com
1-800-Authors (1-800-288-4677)

ISBN: 978-1-4401-4704-3 (sc)
ISBN: 978-1-4401-6564-1 (ebook)

Printed in the United States of America

iUniverse rev. date: 7/21/2009

The painting of John Adams on the cover by Gilbert Stuart Newton is reprinted by courtesy of the Massachusetts Historical Society. It is from an original painting by Gilbert Stuart of John Adams in 1815 when he was nearing 80.

Acknowledgments

To the Massachusetts Historical Society for preserving and publishing *The Adams Papers.* Without their many decades of arduous
work, this small volume would not have been possible.

I would also like to thank Dr. Earl Loomis and Alex Hillenbrand,
who were kind enough to read the manuscript of *John Adams* prior
to publication. Needless to say, they are not responsible for any errors that may remain in the published text, nor are they responsible
for any views or statements with which they may disagree.

JGC

Contents

Chapter One
The Early Years (1735-1758)

"Mighty states and kingdoms change," wrote the young man. "A few people came over to this new world for conscience' sake; this apparently trivial incident may transfer the great seat of empire to America. Our people will, in another century, become more numerous than in England itself. The united force of Europe will not be able to subdue us."

The young man who wrote those words was a twenty-year old school teacher in Worcester, Massachusetts named John Adams. The year was 1755, and at that time America was a group of thirteen relatively unimportant colonies that was part of a great empire ruled by England. To most Europeans it was a wilderness for which England, France, and Spain were still contending.

At the end of the century John Adams spoke of, America had a population more than double that of England and was a free and independent nation. Adams himself had helped forge that nation, had been an architect of its laws and constitutions, both federal and states, and after the long struggle for independence became the new nation's second president. Two centuries later the United States of America was the most powerful nation on earth, a bulwark of freedom and democracy.

John Adams, born in Braintree (the name was changed to Quincy in 1792), Massachusetts on October 19, 1735,[1] was the fifth generation of Adams in this country. His great-great grandfather, Henry Adams, had emigrated to Boston from England in 1636 and settled in Braintree, ten miles south of Boston, in 1640. He, and all his progeny, had been farmers, with the exception of John's uncle, Joseph Adams, who was a minister in New Hampshire.

It was traditional to send the eldest son to college, and John's father, a deacon in the Braintree First Congregational Church and a selectman in the town, had determined that John, *his* eldest son, was to be a minister. The ministry, it was felt, was the highest calling to which a young man could aspire. Ministers were not only spiritual leaders of their communities, but frequently temporal leaders as well. For the pulpit provided a powerful platform for the spread of ideas as well as gospel, and the sermon was considered the most important part of the service.

John, however, had other ideas. As a young boy, he hated school. He wanted to be a farmer like his father. His greatest pleasure, when he found time from chores and his studies, was roaming the countryside for miles around with a gun crooked over his arm, shooting the woodchucks, squirrels, rabbits, and crows that abounded in that section of the country.

One of his favorite walks was to the top of Penn's Hill, which could be seen from their house. Standing there on the granite outcroppings at the top, he could see the sea and, far to the left, Boston Harbor.

---

1 *In 1852, on September 3 (now September 14), England adopted the Gregorian calendar, requiring all dates before that time to be adjusted by plus 11 days to get the dates that now prevail. E.g. the correct date for John Adams' birthday is now October 30.*

Born and raised near the ocean, all his life long he liked to be within sight and sound of it.

The house where John was born and where he lived with his parents and his two younger brothers, Peter and Elihu, was on the main road to Boston. It was of the saltbox variety so typical of New England at that time, with two stories in front and a steep roof that sloped off to one story in the back. A shed John's father had added to the back of the house contained the kitchen and two small rooms where the boys slept. Next door there was a tenant house that Deacon Adams also owned, which was identical to it.

John walked to school each morning, first to Dame Belcher's, the next house down on the other side of the road. There, with the other boys and girls of the town, he received his primary training. Along with the three R's – reading, 'riting, and 'rithmetic – he was given a liberal dose of the Puritan orthodoxy that was his heritage. Even little six-year-old children were thought to be capable of sin, and *The New England Primer* that was their reader contained such "salutary" passages as the following to warn them:

> *There is a hell,*
> *Where wicked ones must always dwell;*
> *There is a heaven full of joy,*
> *Where goodly ones must always stay;*
> *To one of these my soul must fly,*
> *As in a moment, when I die.*

When he was eight or nine, John was transferred to Joseph Cleverly's Latin School. There he developed such a distaste for scholarship that his father despaired of sending him on to Harvard. "You know I have set my heart on your education at college," his father said to him one day when he was fourteen. "Why must you resist?" "Sir," John replied, "I don't like my schoolmaster. He is so negligent and so cross that I never can learn anything under him. If you will be so good as to persuade Mr. Marsh to take me, I will apply myself to my studies as closely as my nature will admit and go to college as soon as I can be prepared."

Joseph Marsh was a local tutor whose father had been a minister in Braintree some years before. Marsh had been in charge of the Latin School before Cleverly, but gave it up because he preferred to teach using his own method and materials. He was known to be an excellent scholar but was suspected of being somewhat liberal in his leanings. However, John's father was desperate and willing to try anything if it would encourage his son to prepare for the career he had planned for him.

The choice turned out to be a fortunate one, for Joseph Marsh was able to light a spark in John Adams for books and scholarship that was not to be dimmed for the rest of his life. Marsh also uncovered and stimulated in the boy an amazing capacity for sheer, dogged hard work. John studied day and night, while the fowling piece he used for hunting lay unused, and the wooded hills changed color, were blanketed with snow, and turned green without his presence among them.

In little more than a year, Marsh had done a thorough job of preparing John for the Harvard entrance exams. When the day came to take them, John rose early and, borrowing his father's horse, set out on the long ride to Cambridge. On the way he stopped by for Mr. Marsh, who was to go with him to introduce him to the Harvard tutors and smooth his path. But Marsh sent down word that he was sick and would be unable to go.

For a time John thought of turning back, for the thought of facing the gowned and wigged President and tutors of the college by himself was almost too much for him. Facing his father, however, would be worse, so he went on, frightened but determined to do his best at the examination.

In Harvard Hall his turn finally came to go before President Edward Holyoke and the four tutors – Henry Flynt, Belcher Hancock, Joseph Mayhew, and Thomas Marsh, a cousin of Joseph Marsh. They asked him a number of questions that would reveal his learning. Finally Mayhew, who would be in charge of John's class if he was admitted, put a passage of English in his hands and asked him to translate it into Latin.

Glancing at it, John was dismayed to see words for which he didn't know the Latin equivalent. But the kindly Mayhew beckoned him into another room and, pointing, said, "There, child, is a dictionary, there a grammar, and there paper, pen and ink, and you may take your own time." Needless to say, "the Latin was soon made" and John was declared admitted.

After a few short weeks of vacation, he returned to enter the freshman class along with twenty-four other boys. The year was 1751 and John was fifteen, going on sixteen. Out of the class of twenty-five, he ranked fifteenth; but at that time students were ranked according to their social backgrounds, not scholarship. In scholarship, John always stood near the top of his class.

Harvard at that time consisted of three red brick buildings in which the student body of about ninety boys ate, slept, and studied. They were built around a quadrangle, and there was a little brick Chapel to the west of the main buildings. The faculty consisted of President Holyoke, a man of liberal and tolerant views (nicknamed "Guts" by the students because of his large stomach), the four tutors, each of whom took one of the classes and lived with the boys in the dormitories, and two professors – Edward Wigglesworth, who taught divinity and the liberal arts, and John Winthrop, who taught science and math.

The typical day began well before sunup. Rising at five, the boys gathered for morning prayers at six, followed by breakfast in their rooms. Classes began at eight with a lecture, by one of the tutors if the boys were freshmen, by one of the professors if they were not. The rest of the day was then spent in study and recitation on the subject of the lecture, with a break for lunch at noon.

Lunch, the main meal of the day, usually consisted of beef or mutton, with beer or cider and hasty pudding or pie for dessert. Afterwards they had an hour or two of free time for play or athletics before returning to their rooms for study. At five they gathered for prayers; supper was at seven-thirty; the bell for bed rang at nine so the students could have adequate time for sleep – but no more.

In his freshman year John studied Greek and Latin, logic, rhetoric, and physics. In his sophomore year the physics was replaced by natural philosophy (a term used at that time for the objective study of the natural world). He began these studies under Professor Winthrop, a leading scientist of his time and a friend to such eminent lights as Benjamin Franklin. In his junior year Adams added moral philosophy, metaphysics, and geography. In his senior year, while reviewing all that he had previously studied, he also studied mathematics and geometry.

Saturdays during the four years were taken up with the study of theology under President Holyoke's tutelage. It should have been John Adams' special concern, but it wasn't; he much preferred science and mathematics. Also, Harvard did not provide the kind of atmosphere that encouraged religious orthodoxy.

Professor Wigglesworth, for example, enjoined his students to think for themselves, at least where doctrine was concerned, and President Holyoke himself once said, "The minister or pastors... have no right to impose their interpretations of the laws of Christ upon their Flocks.... Every man therefore is to judge for himself in these things."

In the summer of 1753 something happened that turned John's thoughts away from the ministry altogether. The young pastor of the First Congregational Church of Braintree, embroiled in a religious controversy with his elders, was charged with being Arminian, Socinian, even Unitarian. It was charged that he denied the Trinity, the Five Points of Calvinism, and the Doctrine of Original Sin. While John took no part in the controversy, he sided with the young pastor, Lemual Briant, and realized that he himself would never be orthodox enough to preach the Scriptures to a Congregational flock.

That spring, too, he read a work that was to have a lasting influence on his mind. It was John Locke's *Essay concerning Human Understanding*. In it he read, "Whilst the parties of man cram their tenets down all men's throats whom they can get into their power, without permitting them to examine their truths or falsehoods, and will not let truth have fair play in the world, nor men the liberty to search after it, what improvement can be expected? What greater light can be hoped for in the moral sciences?" This truth convinced John he could never be a preacher.

When he went back to college that fall, the start of his junior year, he was invited to join the Harvard Discussion Club, which gave him his first taste of public speaking and public applause. His readings from the great tragedies were especially liked. Though absorbed in the private life of college and study, increasing public concern over the French threat to the colonies as the year wore on came to dominate the thinking of John and his fellow students. How could it not? The Boston newspapers were full of it.

During the spring of 1754 French troops invading the colonies from Canada advanced as far south as Lake George in New York and far into Pennsylvania in the west. At the junction of the Ohio and Allegheny Rivers, now the site of Pittsburgh, the French established a large fort and named it Duquesne after the new Governor-General of Canada. Near there, in July, a small band of several hundred Virginia troops under the command of Major George Washington engaged the French and were badly beaten.

In February of 1755, British troops in their bright red coats finally arrived, landing two regiments of regulars under the command of General Braddock in Virginia. Though they would eventually be defeated in a disastrous campaign, their arrival eased the public concern, and John Adams was able to turn his thoughts to his impending graduation.

The happy event took place in July, when friends and relatives of the students, and inhabitants for miles around, gathered for a week of riotous merrymaking. John was one of those chosen to make a commencement address. A Reverend Thaddeus Maccarty of Worcester, who was looking for a schoolteacher, was so impressed with John's learning and eloquence that he hired him on the spot. The next month John began teaching in the Center School in Worcester, a town of fifteen hundred people some fifty miles or so southwest of Boston.

The change in location and the start of a new career should have made him excited and happy. Instead, it was a great disappointment to him. "I heartily sympathize with you in your affliction," he wrote a classmate now pastor in a remote district of New Hampshire. "I am myself confined to a like place of torment. When I compare the gay, the delightsome scenes of Harvard with the harsh and barbarous nature of sounds that now constantly grate my ears I can hardly imagine myself the same being that once revell'd in all the pleasures of an academical life. Total and complete misery has succeeded so suddenly to total and complete happiness, that all the philosophy I can muster can scarce support me under the amazing shock."

But while John found teaching a chore, a veritable prison-house that took up all his time, he was pleased to find himself accepted in the best society of Worcester. He dined frequently with the Chandlers, the leading family of Worcester. There he met many of the town's leading lights, among them a young lawyer by the name of James Putnam, who liked to debate points of theology with the new schoolmaster. Using a lawyer's tactics one evening, Putnam claimed "that the Apostles were a company of enthusiasts. We have," he said, "only their words, to prove that they spoke with different tongues, raised the dead, and healed the sick, etc." It was heresy, but it stimulated John to think about his future career.

A severe earthquake in Braintree in November of that year, one of a series on both sides of the Atlantic that earlier had virtually destroyed the city of Lisbon, shook John awake one morning and started him on the life-long, though intermittent, habit of keeping a diary. In the beginning it was little more than a brief record of the weather and his daily activities and readings, but increasingly it became a vehicle for his thoughts and speculations – about religion, the nature of the universe, and his own character.

In it he frequently chastises himself for his vanity, his laziness, his dullness, and other faults. And on occasion there are touches of self-pity, of which he seems unaware. "All my time seems to roll away unnoticed," he wrote on Saturday, April 24, 1756. "I long to study sometimes but have no opportunity. I long to be a master of Greek and Latin. I long to prosecute the mathematical and philosophical sciences. I long to know a little of ethics and moral philosophy. But I have no books, no time, no friends."

Other entries, however, make it clear that he was a constant reader of both contemporary and classical authors, that books were obviously available to him, and that he had an active social life. One of the libraries open to him was that of Dr. Nahum Willard, with whom John stayed when he first came to Worcester. Willard tried to interest John in becoming a doctor, but medicine was not to his liking. The truth was, he didn't know what he wanted to become, only that he didn't want to remain a schoolteacher all his life. But the ministry seemed definitely out.

He was too much attracted by the views of friends like Ephraim Doolittle and Nathan Baldwin, who were "great readers of deistical books, and very great talkers." Their religious thinking was far from what prevailed at the time. Another friend, Joseph Dyer, was even an outspoken anti-Trinitarian. And even their political thinking was unorthodox. They were all for equality. Dyer went so far as to maintain that "a perfect equality of suffrage was essential to liberty." But John enjoyed their company and spent many an evening with them.

Appreciative of John's intellect, they urged him to become a lawyer. But law, at first, did not attract him, either. He thought of a lawyer as someone who "often foments more quarrels than he composes – and enriches himself at the expense of impoverishing others more honest and deserving than himself." Then something occurred that changed his mind – Court Week in May, when lawyers from miles around came to plead their cases before the Court of Common Pleas in Worcester.

John, who sat in on many of these cases, was fascinated by the drama of the court-room and impressed with the wit, learning, and debating skill of the lawyers. He even envied his friend James Putnam as he watched him in action. It started him thinking seriously about the law, and by August, 1756 the decision was made. A diary entry for Sunday, the twenty-second, tells the whole story:

"Yesterday I completed a contract with Mr. Putnam, to study law under his inspection for two years. Necessity drove me to this determination, but my inclination I think was to preach. However that would not do. But I set out with firm resolutions I think never to commit any meanness or injustice in the practice of law. The study and practice of law, I am sure does not dissolve the obligations of morality or of religion. And although the reason of my quitting divinity was my opinion concerning some disputed points, I hope I shall not give reason of offense to any in that profession by imprudent warmth."

The terms of the contract were that he was to continue teaching, that the town was to pay Mrs. Putnam for his board, and that John was to pay Mr. Putnam a hundred dollars when he found it convenient. That same month England declared war against the French, giving official recognition to the three years of hostilities that had already taken place in the struggle that came to be known, in England, as the Seven Years' War, and, in America as the French and Indian War.

John, however, had little thought to give to the war as he plunged into books on the law, struggling through such ponderous tomes as Sir Edward Coke's *Institutes of the Laws of England* and William Hawkins' *A Treatise of the Pleas of the Crown*. In addition, he did law-clerking for Mr. Putnam, writing simple writs, searching precedents, and following the court sessions.

His studies were temporarily interrupted in the summer of 1757, when he volunteered to ride as a messenger to Rhode Island to arouse Governor Greene to the dangers of the French. The French were about to attack Fort William at the southern end of Lake George, and Thomas Pownall, the new Governor of Massachusetts, had called up twenty-six regiments that were ready to march (Worcester became the temporary headquarters for troops from the middle counties).

On August 3 news of the surrender of Fort Henry, the heaviest military disaster New England had ever suffered, reached Worcester and roused the colonies to their danger. But the following summer the tide began to turn. After eight weeks of fighting between the troops under the commands of General Louis Joseph de Amherst and James Wolfe (a British soldier at the time), the British captured Louisburg a French fort in Nova Scotia.

Meanwhile, John's two years of apprenticeship with Putnam were almost up. In October of 1758 he returned to Braintree, determined to practice law there. First, however, he had to be admitted to practice before the Superior Court.

On Tuesday, October 24, he records in his diary, he rode to Boston and "attended Court steadily all day." The next morning, screwing up his courage, he went to see Jeremiah Gridley, one of Boston's leading lawyers, to ask his advice about what steps he should take to be admitted. Mr. Gridley received him kindly and offered to recommend him to the Court and to speak to the Bar about him, since it would take their consent.

He questioned John about the method of study he had pursued, gave him some materials to read, and then spoke to him like a father. "I have a few pieces of advice, Mr. Adams," he said. "One is to pursue the study of the law rather than the gain of it…. The next is, not to marry early. For an early marriage will obstruct your improvement, and in the next place, will involve you in expense. Another thing is not to keep much company. For the application of a man who aims to be a lawyer must be incessant."

John was to take his advice seriously. The two men then went out to spend the day in Court, and that evening John spoke to Oxenbridge Thacher, another of the legal lights in Boston, to ask his "concurrence with the Bar." Thacher was equally agreeable, though he thought the country was too full of lawyers as it was.

With two conquests under his belt, John went the next morning to see Benjamin Prat, the third of the four men who dominated Boston law. Here he was not so successful. Had he been sworn at Worcester? Prat wanted to know. John had to admit he hadn't. "Have you a letter from Mr. Putnam to the Court?"

Again John had to say no.

"When a young gentleman goes from me into another county," Prat replied, "I always write in his favor to the Court in that county, or if you had been sworn there, you would have been entitled to be sworn here. But now, nobody in this county knows anything about you. So nobody can say anything in your favor, but by hearsay." John went away, he writes in his diary, "full of wrath."

That evening he went to see James Otis, the last member of the quartet, a man Putnam considered the greatest lawyer in Boston. The meeting was brief but fateful. Otis was a brilliant, fiery, passionate man, a great lawyer who later suffered from insanity and died from a stroke of lightning while standing in a farmhouse doorway. Adams was later to consider him, with the exception of George Washington, the greatest man he had ever known. He was also the man who in the famous Writs of Assistance case, John came to believe, struck the first blow for American independence.

In his diary for that evening, John merely noted that they had conversed and that Otis, "with great ease and familiarity, promised me to join the Bar in recommending me to the Court." He returned to Braintree to await the next meeting of the Superior Court, and spent the next four days "in absolute idleness," or what was worse he wrote in his diary, "gallanting the girls."

On November 6, he again rode into Boston, this time to be sworn in with his friend Samuel Quincy. John called twice on Mr. Gridley, but Gridley had not yet returned from Brookline. Finally, John went to the Court by himself "and began to grow uneasy expecting that Quincy would be sworn and I have no patron, when Mr. Gridley made his appearance."

Mr. Gridley whispered something to the other lawyers, and John could hear Mr. Prat say that nobody knew him. "Yes, says Gridley, I have tried him, he is a very sensible fellow."

The two young lawyers were then called forward, recommended to the Court, and took the oath.

Chapter Two
The Young Lawyer (1758-1767)

John Adams' first case as a lawyer was a mortifying failure. It had to do with a neighbor's quarrel over a horse. The horse, belonging to Luke Lambert, had broken into the enclosure of Joseph Field and stayed there for several days eating fodder. As Field was about to drive the horse to the pound, Lambert came along and chased it home. Field sued for damages, but the writ John drew up was defective and the case was thrown out of court.

Field "waxed hot" and "wished the affair in hell," John wrote in his diary. He thought he would never live the case down, that his friends would laugh at him and that an opinion would spread among the people that he had no "cunning." In a self-pitying vein, he continued, "It is my destiny to dig treasures with my own fingers. Nobody will lend me or sell me a pick axe." He took Putnam to task for not having trained him better. But business would have been slow, regardless. People in the smaller country towns saved most of their legal affairs for the warmer months when the Superior Court made its circuit.

John kept himself busy studying, "at least six hours a day," though frequently distracted by such diversions as the town had to offer, and by his own nature. "Laziness, languor, inattention are my bane," he wrote in January of 1759. "I am too lazy to rise early and make a fire, and when my fire is made, at 10 o'clock my passion for knowledge, fame, fortune or any good, is too languid to make me apply with spirit to my books."

One of the principal distractions was a girl by the name of Hannah Quincy, daughter of Colonel Josiah Quincy. John liked her lively nature and was so frequently in her company that their talk skirted the dangerous shoals of matrimony. He and Hannah were having a conversation one day that "would have terminated in a courtship" if his friend Jonathan Sewall and Hannah's cousin Esther had not broken in upon them.

The interruption saved him, John said, from a marriage which "might have depressed me to absolute poverty and obscurity, to the end of my life. But the accident separated us…delivered me from very dangerous shackles, and left me at liberty, if I will mind my studies, of making a character and a fortune.…Reputation ought to be the perpetual subject of my thoughts and aim of my behavior," he admonished himself.

"How shall I gain a reputation! How shall I spread an opinion of myself as a lawyer of distinguished genius, learning, and virtue? … Shall I look out for a cause to speak to, and exert all my soul and all the body I own, to cut a flash, strike amazement, to catch the vulgar? In short, shall I walk a lingering, heavy pace or shall I take one bold determined leap into the midst of some cash and business? That is the question. A bold push, a resolute attempt, a determined enterprise, or a slow, silent, imperceptible creeping. Shall I creep or fly?"

John thought he had found the cause he could fight for in a chance remark of Governor Pownall to the effect that every other house was a tavern. Braintree alone, with a population of about fifteen hundred, had twelve taverns. John even drew a crude map showing their locations. "Here," he wrote, "the time, the money, the health and the modesty of most that are young and of many old, are wasted; here diseases, vicious habits, bastards and legislators are frequently begotten." He called upon the selectmen not to grant approbation, and upon the grand jurors to prosecute the bad houses, and he succeeded in getting all but four of the taverns closed down. But he was dismayed at how little popularity it gained him, and he did not fight it when one by one they reopened.

Another thing that bothered him was the great number of "pettifoggers" there were in the law – people who were not educated for the law, not trained for it, and knew next to nothing about it. On one of his frequent trips to Boston he mentioned the problem to his fellow lawyers. They agreed that the standards of the law needed upgrading and decided to establish an informal club that could meet to discuss what could be done about it.

The club soon attracted all the leading lawyers of Boston to it, and while professional problems formed the main topics of conversation at their meetings, much good humor and learning was displayed. John was to remember many of these meetings in later life as "the most delightful entertainments I ever enjoyed."

Meanwhile, his law practice was slowly building, and the long war between France and England for the continent of North America was drawing toward a conclusion. On July 27, 1759, the English General Sir William Johnson captured Niagara, and two days later the British general Baron Jeffrey Amherst took Ticonderoga. The only French stronghold of any consequence that remained was Quebec.

In preparation for its assault, England sent over the mightiest fleet that had ever crossed the Atlantic, and the following summer forces under the commands of General Louis Joseph de Montcalm and James Wolfe, a British soldier, met on the Plains of Abraham. Montcalm was mortally wounded, and Wolfe was killed. But Quebec fell to the English. On September 8, 1760, Montreal and Canada surrendered, and the Seven Years' (French and Indian) War was finally over, though peace was not signed until 1763.

A few months later something occurred that, although it didn't garner the same headlines, was to have an equally profound influence on the future of the American people. A customs official by the name of James Cockle applied for writs of assistance, in effect general search warrants, that would enable him to search any ship, warehouse, shop, or home for contraband or smuggled goods.

Some Boston merchants felt this was an infringement of their liberties, and fought Cockle's application in the courts. The case finally came to trial in February of 1761, with Jeremiah Gridley acting for the Crown and Oxenbridge Thacher, a student of Gridley's, and James Otis acting for the merchants. John Adams, along with his friend Samuel Quincy, attended the trial and took notes that are our only record of it.

Jeremiah Gridley rose first and spoke for the Crown. He pointed out the necessity of the writs for "assistance" in the proper enforcement of the law and giving the legal basis for them. Oxenbridge Thacher then stood up and replied, also reasoning from the law and precedent. At last James Otis stood up.

While admitting the legality of special writs, Otis argued that a general writ was an infringement of man's basic right to liberty, to be "as secure in his house, as a prince in his castle....An act against the Constitution is void," he exclaimed. "An act against natural equity is void; and if an act of Parliament should be made, in the very words of this petition it would be void."

They were words of defiance. Thrilled, John realized that he was witnessing the first direct confrontation between the English Crown and the American colonists over an issue that was vital to their liberty. Years later, though the case was ultimately decided in favor of the writs, he wrote that it was then "the child independence was born." He claimed it was the day the Revolution began.

A few months later, in May of 1761, an influenza epidemic swept Braintree, and John's father, Deacon John Adams, died at the age of seventy after coming down with it. Of immediate consequence was the fact that John inherited the house next door as his share of the estate. It made him a property owner, a freeholder, and a taxpayer. As such, he was now entitled to vote at the town meetings and to hold office.

His friend Dr. Savil, who occupied the house he inherited, promptly nominated him for the office of Surveyor of Highways and he was elected. It was the first public office Adams had ever held, though without pay. As a monument to his tenure as surveyor, he had a stone bridge built over the stream between the properties of Parson Wibird and Dr. Millar. Unfortunately, it was washed away by floods the next spring. Luckily for John's political reputation, the workmen were blamed and the bridge was rebuilt.

In November John Adams and Samuel Quincy rode into Boston together to be sworn in as barristers before the Superior Court. Such a step enhanced his professional reputation, though it did little to immediately stimulate business, which was still far from satisfactory. One result was that John had time that winter to occasionally ride over to Weymouth with his friend Richard Cranch to visit Parson Smith and his family.

Cranch was courting the eldest daughter, Mary, and John would go along for the ride and because he enjoyed the company of the younger girls in the family, Abigail and Eliza. Abigail, especially, attracted him. Though nine years his junior, she had an intelligence and independence of will that matched his own. Soon he was finding excuses, legal and otherwise, for visits to the Smith family, with or without Cranch.

Head over heels in love, he pressed his suit ardently, and by the summer of 1762 had proposed. He was accepted, but because of Abigail's youth – she was only seventeen – a prolonged engagement of two years was agreed upon. It was a torture to both of them. When a storm delayed his seeing her in February of 1763, he wrote that it was both cruel and blessed, "cruel for detaining me from so much friendly and social company, and perhaps blessed to you, or me or both, for keeping me *at my distance*."

When they were apart they wrote passionate letters to one another. In a self-conscious literary style, he called her Diana and she called him Lysander. Their longest separation occurred in the spring of 1764 when he decided to be inoculated for smallpox. In those days it meant going to a hospital and, after a week of preparation, being given a small case of the pox which resulted in a mild sickness and a long confinement and quarantine.

During his stay in the hospital, they exchanged frequent letters with one another. Their letters were full of love, lightness, and playful teasing. John called her "the dear partner of all my joys and sorrows, in whose affections and friendship I glory, more than in all other emoluments under heaven." When she expressed concern for his recovery, he wrote that he would "unquestionably go to romping very soon" with one of the female patients. Abigail then reproached him for bestowing "those favors upon others which I should rejoice to receive, yet must be deprived of."

At last, in May, the long ordeal was over. There was now the longer ordeal of summer to be gotten through and love's temptations to be resisted. John kept himself busy about the farm – when he wasn't practicing law – building fences, clearing swamps, planting vegetables, and fixing up the house. Abigail, for her part, was busy shopping for furnishings for her home, and was caught up in a round of prenuptial activities. By the time the day finally arrived, they were both close to physical and emotional exhaustion.

On October 25, 1764, they were married in the meeting-house in Weymouth by Abigail's father, Parson William Smith. John then took his new bride home to their own house and farm, settling down to a marriage that was to be one of the most enduring and perfect on record. Meanwhile, events were taking place that were to have a profound effect on the future of the American colonies, and on the future of John and Abigail.

England, searching for ways to help reduce the enormous debt incurred as a result of the recent war, in 1764 passed the American Revenue Act, known in this country as the Sugar Act. It imposed duties on molasses and sugar and a number of other commodities. Massachusetts was immediately up in arms about it. At a noisy town meeting in Boston, James Otis delivered a *Statement of the Rights of the Colonies* in which he declared that taxation without representation was unconstitutional. A committee to correspond with the other colonies was formed and plans laid to embargo certain British goods.

Amidst the furor, word arrived that Parliament was planning to pass a stamp tax, the first direct tax on the colonies, unless the colonies proposed some form of self-taxation to help raise the needed revenue. The colonies, however, showed no signs of imposing a tax on themselves, and on March 8, 1765, the Stamp Act passed both houses of Parliament. It provided for a tax, to be indicated by a stamp, on legal documents, newspapers, licenses, and other printed matter.

The reaction in the colonies was immediate and virulent. When the stamps finally arrived they were seized and burned and crowds surged through the streets of Boston crying, "No taxation without representation!" On August 14 crowds sacked the home of the Boston distributor of the stamps, Andrew Oliver, and burned him in effigy. A few days later the home of Lieutenant Governor Thomas Hutchinson was also gutted.

John Adams deplored the mob's violence but, caught up in the excitement of the times, wrote an essay for the Boston *Gazette* called "A dissertation on Canon and Feudal Law." Nowhere near as dry as the title sounds, it was an impassioned plea for freedom. It traced the rise of freedom and showed how it might be maintained and extended. "There are Rights," he wrote, "that cannot be repealed or restrained by human law – Rights derived from the great Legislator of the universe." Education and a free press are essential supports of a free people. "The true source of our sufferings has been our timidity. We have been afraid to think…. The fact is certain, we have been excessively cautious in giving offense by complaining of grievances." The articles were unsigned, but the author soon became known.

Adams was moved to action as well as words. The General Court of Massachusetts was to meet in October to take up the question of the Stamp Act, and John felt that the Braintree representative, Ebenezer Thayer, ought to be instructed on what stand to take. He accordingly petitioned the selectmen for a town meeting, drew up a set of instructions, and got them accepted. Among the points he made was that "we have always understood it to be a grand and fundamental principle of the constitution, that no freeman should be subject to any tax to which he has not given his own consent, in person or by proxy." Thayer was enjoined not to comply with the Stamp Act and to resist its execution.

The Braintree Instructions, as they were called, were widely circulated and came to be adopted by many of the towns in Massachusetts. They were dated September 24, 1765.

On December 18 Adams commented in his diary: "That enormous engine, fabricated by the British Parliament, for battering down all the rights and liberties of America, I mean the Stamp Act, has raised and spread, through the whole continent, a spirit that will be recorded to our honor, with all future generations. In every colony, from Georgia to New Hampshire inclusively, the Stamp distributors and inspectors have been compelled, by the unconquerable rage of the people, to renounce their offices."

Without the stamps, all legal business came to a standstill. John, with a growing family to provide for (a daughter, named Abigail after his wife and nicknamed Nabby, had been born on July 14, 1765), felt the pinch acutely. "This long interval of indolence and idleness," he wrote, "will make a large chasm in my affairs, if it should not reduce me to distress and incapacitate me to answer the demands upon me." In a burst of self-pity, he added, "Thirty years of my life are passed in preparation for business. I have had poverty to struggle with – envy and jealously and malice of enemies to encounter – no friends, or but few to assist me, so that I have groped in dark obscurity, till of late, and had but just become known, and gained a small degree of reputation, when this execrable project was set on foot for my ruin as well as that of America in general, and of Great Britain," ignoring the fact that others were feeling the pinch as well.

The very next day Adams received a letter notifying him that he had been voted unanimously by the Town of Boston to appear as counsel, along with Jeremiah Gridley and James Otis, "before his Excellency the Governor in Council, in support of their memorial, praying that the courts of law in this province may be opened." It was a signal honor for a young country lawyer, and undoubtedly reflected the impression his Instructions and Dissertation had made on the legal fraternity. Adams, affecting false modesty, claimed not to know "the reasons which induced Boston to choose me, at a distance, and unknown as I am."

He had a scant twenty-four hours to prepare his case. The next evening, after a brief dinner meeting with Otis and Gridley, they went before the Governor. Adams, surprised at being called on first, grounded his "argument on the invalidity of the Stamp Act, it not being in any sense our act, having never consented to it. But lest that foundation should not be sufficient, on the present necessity to prevent a failure of justice, and the present impossibility of carrying that act into execution." When he was done, Otis "reasoned with great learning and zeal, on the judges' oaths, etc.," and "Mr. Gridley on the great inconveniences that would ensue the interruption of justice."

The Governor was not swayed, and the Council adjourned. When informed of the Governor's answer, the Town of Boston voted unanimously that it was not satisfactory, and the deadlock continued. The colonies, at a congress in New York in October, had drawn up a petition to the House of Commons, an address to the King, and thirteen resolves. There was nothing to do now but wait for a reply that was slow in coming.

With time on his hands, Adams wrote a series of articles for the Boston *Gazette* on the British constitution and American rights, the so-called "Clarendon Letters." Their tone was moderate but firm, and they added to his already increasing reputation. Because of this, and his Stamp Act activities, Adams found many doors in Boston open to him, and he spent much time there.

He was an especial favorite of the Sons of Liberty, a patriotic organization that had been formed the previous summer by Otis and Samuel Adams, a distant cousin of John's, to lead many of the anti-government demonstrations. In Braintree, John had also become something of a celebrity, so much so that at their annual town meeting in March of 1766 they elected him a selectman.

On May 19, word reached Boston that the Stamp Act had been repealed. There was wild rejoicing, though John, on his way to Plymouth to attend court the next day, missed most of it. "The only rejoicing I heard or saw," he wrote, "were at Hingham, where the bells rung, cannons were fired, drums beaten, and Land Lady Cushing on the plain illuminated her house."

With the repeal of the hated tax, John's law business grew by leaps and bounds. He was so busy with his practice, his duties as selectman, and with farm and family concerns, that he had little thought to give to politics. The money he earned he spent on land and books. In March he was re-elected selectman, and on July 11, 1767, Abigail gave birth to their second child, a son they named John Quincy after Abigail's grandfather.

Chapter Three
The Revolutionary (1767-1774)

The period of calm that followed the repeal of the Stamp Act did not last long – little more than a year. The friction between the mother country and the colonies began to heat up again when, in May of 1767, England's new Chancellor of the Exchequer, Charles Townshend, proposed three acts dealing with American affairs. One was a revenue act imposing duties on certain goods imported into the colonies, notably glass, lead, paints, tea, and paper. Parliament passed these acts, known as the Townshend Acts, in June.

To the colonists it was the same old story of taxation without representation. Patriots everywhere, including John Adams, were incensed. On October 28, a few weeks before the first taxes were to be collected, Boston held a town meeting with James Otis as moderator. It was voted not to import or use any of the duadied articles, and committees were appointed to urge the merchants to comply and to correspond with the other colonies to get them to agree to non-importation.

With all the political excitement in the air, John found it increasingly difficult to keep his mind on his business. On January 30, 1768, a Saturday night, he wrote in his diary: "To what object are my views directed? What is the end and purpose of my studies, journeys, labors of all kinds of body and mind, of tongue and pen? Am I grasping at money, or scheming for power? Am I planning the illustration of my family or the welfare of my country?"

His decision to move to Boston shortly after that was his answer. While it would undoubtedly be good for business, Boston was a political center that drew him like a magnet. In March he declined to run for reelection as a selectman of Braintree, and in April he packed up his goods and moved with Abigail and the two children into a house on Brattle Square. It was in the very heart of town, only a few blocks from Faneuil Hall and the State House.

The move was made in the midst of a political uproar. In February the General Court had sent a circular letter drafted by Samuel Adams to the legislative assemblies of the other colonies informing them of the steps being taken to fight the Townshend Acts. Angrily denouncing this action as seditious, Governor Francis Bernard dissolved the General Court and wrote to England for instructions.

Lord Hillsborough, Secretary for the Colonies, replied with a demand that the letter be rescinded. A special General Court called for that purpose defiantly voted 92 to 17 not to rescind. Throughout the colonies, the 92 immediately became heroes and the 17 were hissed as "slaves." To commemorate the occasion, Paul Revere fashioned a silver punch bowl inscribed with the words: "To the Glorious 92, who ignoring the insolent menaces of villains in power, voted **NOT TO RESCIND.**"

Meanwhile, the customs officials in Boston, because of the uproar over the duties, with mobs gathering in the streets, were concerned for their personal safety. They wrote to England for help, and General Gage, the commander-in-chief of the British forces in America, was ordered to protect them and enforce the laws. A British frigate, the *Romney*, was dispatched from Halifax.

The frigate arrived in Boston harbor early in June 1768. Taking advantage of its presence, the customs officials ordered John Hancock's sloop, the *Liberty*, seized and held for its refusal to pay import duties on some Madeira wine that had been unloaded illegally. This would be an important test case because Hancock, one of the richest merchants in Boston, was also the prime financial backer of the patriots.

The mob that formed when the people heard of the seizure descended on the customs officials and forced them to flee to the sanctuary of Castle William, a government fort in the harbor. Amidst rumors that British troops would be called to restore order, the people of Boston met in a town meeting that overflowed Faneuil Hall. There, with James Otis as moderator, they voted to petition the Governor to have the *Romney* removed. They also named John Adams to a committee to draw up instructions for the four newly elected representatives to the General Court.

John immediately set to work. Noting with regret the bitterness existing between England and the colonies, he listed the presence of the *Romney*, the removal of the *Liberty*, the impressments of sailors, and the rumor of the importation of troops as issues that should concern them. He also advised the representatives that "it is our unalterable resolution, at all times to assert and vindicate our dear and invaluable rights and liberties, at the utmost hazard of our lives and fortunes."

Unanimously adopted on July 17, Adams' instructions did much to rally the colonists to the common cause. But few people knew what a sacrifice these words cost him. About the time he was writing them, his old friend Jonathan Sewall called on him with an offer from Governor Bernard. The office of Advocate General in the Court of Admiralty was vacant and the Governor wanted to appoint him to that post. The office was lucrative "and a sure introduction to the most profitable business in the province," John wrote. "What was of more consequence still," he continued, "it was a first step in the ladder of royal favor and promotion."

John, however, turned him down. When Sewall asked why, Adams replied that "he knew very well my political principles, the system I had adopted and the connections and friendships I had formed in consequence of them. He also knew that the British government, including the King, his ministers and Parliament, apparently supported by a great majority of the nation, were persevering in a system, wholly inconsistent with all my ideas of right, justice and policy, and therefore I could not place myself in a situation in which my duty and my inclination would be so much at variance."

Instead of acting for the Crown, Adams was engaged by Hancock to defend him against the charge of smuggling in the case of the *Liberty*. If he lost, Hancock would be subject to the enormous sum of 9,000 pounds, three times the value of the cargo, but vastly more important would be the blow to the patriot cause of which Hancock had become the symbol.

Possibly because of the public agitation, the Crown waited until October when Boston had been occupied by British troops before filing its suit, and it announced that the case would be tried by an admiralty court, not a jury. For Adams the case proved to be a "painful drudgery" that dragged on through the winter, with the Crown seemingly determined to examine the whole town as witnesses. He put up a stubborn defense, questioning the validity of legislation that denied his client trial by jury. On March 25, 1769, the Crown's attorneys admitted defeat and dropped the charge.

That case was hardly out of the way, however, when another came his way that was to arouse equal public excitement. Four American sailors were charged with murdering a British naval officer by the name of Lt. Henry Gibson Panton, and Adams was retained to defend them. The story was that Panton had intercepted and boarded the American brig *Pitt* on its way from Calais to Marblehead and tried to impress the sailors. The sailors hid in the hold, and when Panton went in after them, they threw a harpoon at him that severed his jugular vein.

Impressment of American sailors by the British had long been a sore point with the colonists, and the case aroused the keenest interest. Actually, there was a little-known law against impressment, and when it became apparent to the judges that Adams was going to bring it up, they promptly adjourned. The next day they brought in a verdict of not guilty by reason of self-defense to avoid the whole issue.

Both these cases added greatly to Adams' growing reputation. His law practice increased so rapidly he was soon one of the busiest lawyers in Boston. Much of his time was spent "riding circuit" – attending court in small towns as far north as Falmouth and as far south as Plymouth. While he enjoyed these trips, he also felt much apprehension at leaving Abigail and the two children in Boston alone. Daily, British troops paraded in front of his house, and the tension between the troops and the populace was such that any day it might erupt into violence.

Returning to town from a brief trip to Weymouth at the end of February 1770, Adams came upon a vast funeral procession for a young boy killed by a customs employee. The employee, Ebenezer

Richardson, had fired his musket blindly into a group of boys who were taunting him at his house for having come to the aid of a merchant known to have violated the non-importation agreement. The incident was a prelude to greater violence.

Only a month later, on March 5, Adams was at a club meeting at the south end of Boston when "about nine o'clock, we were alarmed with the ringing of bells, and supposing it to be the signal of fire, we snatched our hats and cloaks, broke up the club, and went out to assist in quenching the fire or aiding our friends who might be in danger. In the street we were informed that the British soldiers had fired on the inhabitants, killed some and wounded others near the Town house."

Adams went to the spot, but all was quiet and he went home. What had happened was that a lone British sentry in front of the custom-house had been attacked by a mob and had called for help. A squad of seven soldiers came to his aid, and was soon joined by the officer of the day, a Captain Thomas Preston. The mob started stoning and clubbing the soldiers, and one of the soldiers was knocked down. In the confusion, a shot was fired, then six others. Three people dropped dead in the snow and eight others were wounded.

The Boston Massacre, as it was soon called, fanned the feelings of the people to white heat. They poured in from the outlying communities the next morning and a meeting was hastily called by the Sons of Liberty in Faneuil Hall. At the meeting it was voted that a demand be sent to Lt. Governor Hutchinson that the troops be removed from Boston.

That same morning, Adams was visited in his office by a Mr. James Forrest, who came in "with tears streaming from his eyes." He said, "I am come with a very solemn message from a very unfortunate man, Captain Preston in prison. He wishes for counsel, and can get none." Captain Preston and the eight soldiers were to be charged with murder. If Adams didn't take the case, there would be none to defend them.

With full knowledge that the case might cost him his friends and his practice, Adams replied that if Preston "thinks he cannot have a fair trial of that issue without my assistance, without hesitation he shall have it." Mr. Forrest then pressed a guinea into Adams' hand and the bargain was struck. While the decision occasioned much scandal, the faith of the people in Adams' integrity was shown, during the term of the trial, when, in June, they elected him as one of the representatives from Boston to the General Court of Massachusetts.

"I went down to Faneuil Hall," he wrote many years later, "and in a few words expressive of my sense of the difficulty and danger of the times; of the importance of the trust, and of my own insufficiency to fulfill the expectations of the people, I accepted the choice. Many congratulations were offered, which I received civilly, but they gave me no joy." Then, in words rife with the self-indulgence to which he was often prey, he continued:

"I considered the step as a devotion of my family to ruin and myself to death, for I could scarce perceive the possibility that I should ever go through the thorns and leap all the precipices before me, and escape with my life. At this time I had more business at the Bar than any man in the province. My health was feeble. I was throwing away as bright prospects as any man ever had before him, and had devoted myself to endless labor and anxiety if not to infamy and to death, and that for nothing, except, what indeed was and ought to be all in all, a sense of duty."

Because of the passions of the populace, the trials of Captain Preston and the eight soldiers were put off until the fall term of Court. Even so, the eyes of all Boston focused on the Town House when the trials finally opened. In the case of Captain Preston, the prosecution was unable to prove that an order had been given to fire and he was acquitted. The trial of the soldiers three weeks later was a little more difficult. Blood was shed and it was felt that someone must pay.

Because of Adams' skillful defense, six were acquitted and two found guilty of the lesser charge of manslaughter. They were let off with a branding on the thumb and sent back to their regiments which, because of the popular clamor, had been removed to Castle William. It was, of course, a signal victory for the defense.

The heavy burdens Adams was bearing, both in private practice and in his duties as a legislator, eventually affected his health. They caused, he wrote, "a pain in my breast and a complaint in my lungs, which seriously threatened my life." Allowing for the usual exaggerations of the hypochondriac, there was no doubt he was run-down. As a result he decided to give up what he felt was the unfavorable air of Boston.

In April 1771 he moved his family back to Braintree, while retaining an office in town. The return to his native soil, to the cares of the farm, and riding the circuit once again soon revived him. He was pleased to renew old friendships and found pleasure in his growing family. A second son, Charles Francis, had been born on May 29, 1770, and a third son, Thomas Boylston, was born on September 15, 1772. They helped to alleviate somewhat the grief occasioned by the death of an infant daughter, Susanna, born less than two years before, in February of 1770.

Farm, family, and a country practice did not satisfy Adams for long, however. Though the patriot cause had waned, he still felt out of things. In November 1772 he moved his family back to Boston. They were hardly settled in their new house in Queen Street before John was thick in the midst of the reviving political quarrel.

Word reached Boston that the Crown proposed to pay the salaries of the judges instead of the people. This meant, of course, that the judges would be dependent on England for their bread as well as their appointments. The patriots, aware that he who pays the piper calls the tune, saw this as a serious threat to the judges' independence. At a special town meeting in Boston on December 14, instructions were voted condemning the proposal.

A General William Brattle, who rose to talk against the instructions, challenged Adams, Otis, and Josiah Quincy to dispute the issue with him, and subsequently published a newspaper article on the subject. John felt constrained to take up the challenge. He published a series of weekly articles in the Boston *Gazette* starting in January 1773 in rejoinder to Brattle. Citing numerous legal authorities, Adams carefully pointed out the dangers of having a judiciary dependent on the Crown.

Meanwhile, more fuel was added to the fire by an inflammatory speech of Governor Hutchinson before the General Court at the beginning of its winter term in January. He stated that Parliament had every right to impose its laws and taxes on the colonies. The reaction and counter-reaction this evoked went on for several months.

In the midst of all the hubbub, word reached Boston that the East India Company was planning to ship an enormous quantity of tea to the colonies. While most of the duties of the Townshend Act had been revoked, the tax on tea had not. Patriots everywhere had sedulously avoided drinking the stuff, or at least paying tax on it since the tax was enacted.

In November the dreaded shipment finally arrived in Boston Harbor. A town meeting was hastily called to determine how they could prevent its being landed. The next few weeks saw a clash of wills between the Governor and the people. Deputations of citizens persuaded the captains of the British ships to return to England without unloading the tea, but Governor Hutchinson refused them the clearance to leave.

On December 16, 1773, a huge meeting was called by the Sons of Liberty at the Old South Meeting House. The meeting was attended by an estimated 7,000 persons, the largest town meeting in Boston's history. While the crowd was harangued by Samuel Adams, Josiah Quincy, and John Rowe, Captain Rotch of one of the tea ships was sent to the Governor to make one last appeal.

When the captain returned with word that clearance had been denied, Samuel Adams announced to the crowd that "This meeting can do nothing more to save the country." As if it were a signal, a group of citizens dressed as Indians whooped past the windows of the meeting house and headed down to Griffin's wharf where the three ships of tea were anchored. They boarded the ships and, working swiftly, in three hours had dumped every chest of tea overboard into the harbor.

When John heard about "The Boston Tea Party" (as it was soon called) the next day, after returning from court at Plymouth, it thrilled him to the bones. He called it "the most magnificent movement of all. "There is a dignity," he continued, "a majesty, a sublimity, in this last effort of the patriots that I greatly admire. The people should never rise without doing something to be remembered – something notable and striking. This destruction of the tea is so bold, so daring, so firm, intrepid and inflexible, and it must have so important consequences, and so lasting, that I can't but consider it as an epoch in history."

He then went on to wonder what steps England would take in retaliation and whether the patriots might have acted differently. There was, he felt, no alternative to destroying the tea or letting it be landed. And "to let it be landed would be giving up [to] the principle of taxation by Parliamentary authority, against which the Continent have struggled for ten years."

When word of the Tea Party reached England, the reaction was vehement. This time, it was felt, the colonies had gone too far. The King, in an address to Parliament early in March 1774, declared that Britain must either master the colonies "or totally leave them to themselves and treat them as aliens."

In the angry debates that followed, one Member cried out that "the town of Boston ought to be knocked down about their ears and destroyed.... You will never meet with proper obedience to the laws of this country until you have destroyed that nest of locusts." And that seemed to be the intention of Parliament.

The first thing they did was to pass a bill closing the port of Boston to all trade and removing the seat of government to Salem. It was the first of five regulatory measures that in America received the title of the "Intolerable Acts" or "Coercive Acts." The severity of these Acts only stiffened patriot resistance. The Committees of Correspondence became active again and word soon flowed into Boston of strong support from the interior towns of Massachusetts and from the other colonies. Pennsylvania, New York City, and Virginia passed resolves condemning the Boston Port Act and calling for action that had the ring of rebellion to it.

The Massachusetts Assembly, meeting in Salem, hastily passed a resolution calling for a Continental Congress of the colonies to meet in September in Philadelphia to discuss what measures might be taken for the relief of Boston and to "plan for a more lasting accommodation with Great Britain." They elected five delegates from Massachusetts: James Bowdoin, Samuel Adams, Thomas Cushing, Robert Treat Paine, and John Adams.

Chapter Four
The Continental Congress (1774-1776)

Meeting Adams at Falmouth, Jonathan Sewall tried one last time to dissuade his friend from the patriot cause. By attending this Continental Congress, Adams, he said, was running the risk of being charged with treason and ruining a brilliant career.

"I have passed the Rubicon," John replied. "Swim or sink, live or die, survive or perish with my country – that is my unalterable determination." And the Rubicon was indeed passed.

On August 10, 1774, the delegates, minus James Bowdoin, who declined to serve, set out from Thomas Cushing's house in Boston accompanied by a large escort of patriots who saw them off. All along the way on the long trip through Connecticut and New York, they were met by large crowds of citizens, and wined and dined by leading patriots.

They arrived in Philadelphia, then the largest city in America with an estimated 25-30,000 inhabitants, on Monday, August 29, exactly a week before Congress was to convene. During that week they were swept up in a round of activities, meeting and getting acquainted with the other delegates, sightseeing, and dining with some of Philadelphia's leading citizens. At ten o'clock on Monday morning, September 6, the assembled delegates met at the City Tavern and walked to the newly-erected Carpenters' Hall nearby, where, after inspecting the rooms, they agreed to meet.

They immediately settled down to business. Peyton Randolph of Virginia was elected Chairman and Charles Thomson, "the Sam Adams of Philadelphia" as John called him, Secretary. There was then a discussion of the rules. Patrick Henry of Virginia pointed out they should be wary of what they do, since they would be setting a precedent for other general Congresses that would surely follow. The delegates agreed they should vote by colony and that each day's meeting should be opened with a prayer.

Two committees were then appointed. The task of the first committee was to "state the rights of the colonies in general, the several instances in which these rights are violated or infringed, and the means most proper to be pursued for obtaining a restoration of them." The task of the second committee was to examine the statutes affecting the trade and manufactures of the colonies.

John Adams was one of the delegates appointed to the important first committee, which immediately began a discussion of the basic rights of the colonies. All members agreed on the principle of no taxation without representation. But was this to be based on the British constitution or on the natural rights of man?

Joseph Galloway of Pennsylvania, a conservative, advanced the revolutionary idea that the colonists were exempt from all the laws passed by Parliament since the migration of the colonists. In fact, he said, "all the acts of Parliament made since are violations of our rights."

On the second day, Patrick Henry declared that "the distinction between Virginians, Pennsylvanians, New Yorkers and New Englanders are no more. I am not a Virginian, but an American." Where would such thinking lead? To many of the delegates, this was dangerous thinking. They were not there to form a union of the colonies, but to seek an accommodation with the "Mother Country," as many referred to England.

Adams came to hate the very sound of those words, "Mother Country," and did all he could to have them stricken from the reports of any committee he worked on. There were other delegates who felt the same way. On the lips of some and in the minds of others, they were increasingly replaced by another word – "independence." But to most of the delegates, this was a radical, a frightening, idea. They wanted merely to establish their rights.

To begin the process, on September 9 they appointed Adams, who had quickly established himself as one of the delegates most versed in the law, to a sub-committee to draw up a statement of those rights. But Congress met its first test, as far as Adams was concerned, on September 16, when Paul Revere delivered the Suffolk County Resolves.

These resolves, drawn up by Joseph Warren (a doctor who died in the Battle of Bunker Hill) and passed by the people of Boston and the surrounding towns, declared that the coercive acts passed by Great Britain were unconstitutional and need not be obeyed. The resolves also advised the people of Massachusetts to arm, and recommended the policy of non-importation.

At the time, the resolves went much further than conservatives of the Continental Congress were willing to go. The radicals, against much opposition, got them approved and supported unanimously, which pleased Adams no end. "This," he recorded in his diary, "was one of the happiest days of my life. In Congress we had generous, noble sentiments, and manly eloquence. This day convinced me that America will support Massachusetts or perish with her."

On September 22 the report of the Committee for Stating Rights and Grievances was read and debated paragraph by paragraph. John Adams was then given the assignment of putting the Declaration of Rights in final shape, while John Sullivan of New Hampshire drew up the Declaration of Violations of Rights. These two Declarations became the basis, two years later, for the sentiments expressed in the Declaration of Independence by Thomas Jefferson.

Congress next turned its attention to the question of non-importation. Richard Henry Lee of Virginia put it in the form of a motion on September 26, and the agreement not to import from either England or Ireland was passed the next day. The only debate was when it should take effect.

This matter was hardly out of the way when Joseph Galloway proposed a political union between the colonies and Great Britain. The trouble with Galloway's plan of union was that it conceded to England many more rights than the patriots cared to forfeit, and it was narrowly defeated by a vote of six colonies to five.

Adams countered with a proposal that all the colonies should support Massachusetts and Boston in their struggle "by every necessary means, and to the last extremity." But this was too much for most of the delegates and, after a brief debate, the motion was set aside.

With the Declaration of Rights and Grievances out of the way, Adams was named to a committee to draw up a petition to the King. While he worked on this, the main body of Congress debated the rights of Parliament to regulate colonial trade. However, the colonies were divided on the issue and no motion was passed. Congress then turned to a consideration of Articles of Association.

These were passed by a majority on October 18. They restated the principal grievances of the colonies, spelled out the policy of non-importation – to be followed by non-exportation at the end of a year if their grievances were still not redressed, and recommended that "Associations" of citizens be formed in every county, city, and town to take action against all merchants or others who violated the articles.

The Declaration of Rights and Grievances, the Nonimportation Agreement, and the Articles of Association were the principal achievements of the first Continental Congress. The members dissolved themselves on Wednesday, October 26, after the petition to the King was debated and passed. John Adams then headed home to Braintree, "with a reputation," he wrote later, "much higher than ever I enjoyed before or since."

The Continental Congress could have been the consummation of John Adams' political career. Instead, it was just the beginning. Upon his return to Braintree, he was promptly elected to the Provincial Congress. Because Boston was still heavily invested with British troops, the Congress met at Cambridge. It could do little but issue proclamations. Still, it remained a focus, in Massachusetts, of the colonists' determination to resist British repression.

It took two significant steps before it dispersed in December. It agreed first of all to raise a force of 12,000 men from Massachusetts to help meet the British threat. And, second, it elected five more delegates to attend a second Continental Congress scheduled to convene in Philadelphia on May 10, 1776. The delegates elected were John Adams, Samuel Adams, Robert Treat Paine, John Hancock, and Thomas Cushing.

John Adams

About this time a series of brilliant Tory articles over the pen name "Massachusettensis" appeared in one of the Boston newspapers. Adams suspected they were written by his friend Jonathan Sewall, though they were actually written by Daniel Leonard. He discovered in them, he wrote, "a subtlety of art and address wonderfully calculated to keep up the spirits of their party, to depress ours, to spread intimidation and to make proselytes among those whose principles and judgment give way to their fears."

As week after week passed and no one took up the pen to reply to them, Adams wrote "these papers made a very visible impression on many minds." Worried about the consequences, he began a series of articles in the Boston *Gazette* in reply to them. The first of them appeared on January 23, 1775, under the signature "Novanglus" (New England). They continued until the battle of Lexington on April 19 which, John wrote, "changed the instruments of warfare from the pen to the sword."

The Novanglus papers traced the history of the conflict between Great Britain and the colonies, detailing the events that led to the Continental Congress. Adams then presented a strong lawyer's brief for the patriot cause, citing precedent and relevant cases. They were, in fact, the ablest and most complete argument for the colonists' position that had appeared up to that time, and they had a great influence.

The last Novanglus essay never appeared, for on April 19 a regiment of British soldiers, on their way to Concord to confiscate a cache of colonial powder, were met by a group of minutemen on the common at Lexington. Though no one knew who fired the "shot heard round the world," more shots were exchanged, and men fell dead and wounded. The British continued their march to Concord, but were forced, finally, to retreat to Boston, swarming minutemen sniping at them from ambush the whole way.

The commencement of hostilities gave to the delegates assembled in the State House in Philadelphia on May 10 for the second Continental Congress a particular sense of urgency. To Adams, "the members appeared...to be of one mind, and that mind after my own heart." Yet, when he stood up and advocated "that we ought to declare the colonies free, sovereign and independent states," he saw "horror, terror and detestation strongly marked on the countenances of some of the members."

John Dickinson of Pennsylvania made a motion for a second petition to the King, and Adams made a long harangue against it. Immediately afterwards, when Adams was called out into the State House yard, Dickinson darted out after him.

"What is the reason, Mr. Adams," he exclaimed, "that you New Englandmen oppose our measures of reconciliation?... Look ye! If you don't concur with us in our pacific system, I and a number of us will break off from you in New England, and we will carry on the opposition by ourselves in our own way."

But the split among the delegates (loyalists and revolutionaries, as they were to become known), never developed in the Congress. There were too many pressing matters to be taken care of. Concessions were made on either side, and the business of Congress proceeded.

One of the first questions to be taken up was that of a commander-in-chief for the Continental forces gathered outside of Boston. Aware of strong Southern feelings and the need to unify the colonies, Adams nominated Colonel George Washington of Virginia. After considerable lobbying on his behalf, he was unanimously elected on June 15, and left soon after to take charge of the ragged New England forces. By this act, Congress took the Continental forces under its wing and voted to raise money for their support. Before Washington could assume command, however, the first major engagement of the war took place.

Learning that the English were about to seize Dorchester Heights just outside of Boston, 1,200 Massachusetts militiamen, led by Colonel William Prescott, secretly occupied and fortified Breed's Hill overlooking Charlestown on the night of June 16 as a countermeasure. The next day, when the English discovered what had happened, they immediately sent 2,400 troops under the command of General Sir William Howe to retake the hill. Twice during the day the English charged, but each time they were driven back with heavy losses. Finally, toward evening, with their ammunition exhausted, the Americans withdrew in the face of a final charge.

The "Battle of Bunker Hill," as it was called, though most of the engagement took place on Breed's Hill, thrilled the colonists as they had never been thrilled before. The brave American troops had stood up to the British redcoats and given them worse than they had received. It made one proud to be an American.

On July 7, Congress adopted "a Declaration of the Causes and Necessity of Taking up Arms," stating that "the arms we have been compelled by our enemies to assume, we will...employ for the preservation of our liberties, being with one mind resolved to die free men than to live slaves."

While Congress was taking vigorous measures to prosecute the war – establishing an army and a general staff, beginning the long struggle to establish an adequate supply system, issuing the first Continental money, and proposing a plan of confederation among the colonies – the forces of moderation were also hard at work. On July 8, John Dickinson's second, or "Olive Branch," petition to the King was passed by Congress.

Adams signed it with disgust, calling it a "measure of imbecility [that] embarrassed every exertion of Congress." By the end of July Congress, "much fatigued with the incessant labors, debates, intrigues, and heats of summer" agreed on a short adjournment. Adams hurried home, not to Braintree but to Watertown, where the Provincial Congress was meeting. He and the other delegates who had been elected to the Council took their seats "for such times as we could spare before our return to Congress."

During that time, in August, Adams had the sad duty of burying his brother Elihu. He also visited the Army and the General Court before returning to Philadelphia on September 12. At this session of Congress Adams found that "every important step was opposed, and carried by bare majorities." This obliged him, he wrote, "to be almost constantly engaged in debate." He spoke out frequently to oppose such conciliatory measures as the petition, and to advise the states to institute governments.

"We ought now," he said, "to be employed in preparing a plan of confederation for the colonies, and treaties to be proposed to foreign powers, particularly to France and Spain, that all these measures ought to be maturely considered, and carefully prepared, together with a declaration of independence."

Congress, however, was not disposed to move that fast. Several weeks were taken up with a consideration of trade and treaties with foreign nations. Adams felt strongly that "we ought not to enter into any alliance...which should entangle us in any future wars in Europe." He felt that a strictly commercial treaty with France, for instance, would be enough to compensate her for any help she gave the colonies.

His speech on the subject met with great attention and approbation from the other members. Even Dickinson conceded that he "had thrown great light on the subject." The final outcome of the debate on trade was that there was to be no trade before March 1 of the following year without the express permission of Congress and that American ports were to remain closed. The next question was what to do about British shipping. Should American ships be turned loose to prey upon it?

Considering the might of the British navy, some members thought the proposition absurd, while the moderates of Congress felt it would be another irreconcilable step toward a final break with the mother country. Adams' view was the most extreme of all: he was in favor of establishing an American navy. The matter was brought to a head when news reached Congress on October 5 that two British sloops loaded with arms and powder had left England and were headed toward Quebec.

Congress promptly named Adams to a committee to decide what action should be taken. The committee recommended that the two brigs be intercepted and that the States of Massachusetts, Connecticut, and Rhode Island turn over armed vessels for commissioning. It produced a heated debate, but was approved by Congress the same day. However humble, it was the beginnings of a navy and gave Adams much satisfaction.

Three weeks later Adams was appointed to a committee authorized to purchase and equip vessels "for the protection and defense of the united colonies." And on November 28, Congress approved "Rules for the Regulation of the Navy of the United Colonies of North American." Another problem that Adams felt was of the utmost urgency was the establishment of state governments.

On October 18 the New Hampshire delegates had asked the Congress for advice on administering justice and regulating the civil police. Adams took the occasion to urge Congress to recommend to the states that such governments be instituted. But the furthest Congress would go was to recommend to New Hampshire, and to South Carolina, which had requested similar advice, that they set up governments "during the continuance of the present dispute." This left open the question of what kind of government.

At the request of Richard Henry Lee of Virginia, Adams submitted his own ideas in writing on November 15. He was, he said, for a balanced government of three equal branches – a legislative, a judicial, and an executive. Each would act as a check on the others. When other delegates asked for similar advice, Adams developed his ideas further and eventually published them in an essay called *Thoughts on Government*. It was widely circulated and had a great influence on the colonies in setting up their individual "state" governments along the lines Adams had suggested.

Another essay published during that winter of 1775-76 was to have even greater impact. This was a pamphlet called *Common Sense* by a renegade Englishman named Thomas Paine. In ringing, eloquent terms, it was a clarion call for independence. It passed avidly from hand to hand, winning many converts to the cause and crystallizing the thinking of both Congress and the people. If Adams found fault with it, it was only because the kind of government suggested ran counter to his own ideas of the government to be set up, and because he felt its reasoning was specious.

Despite the public enthusiasm for independence aroused by *Common Sense*, many members of Congress still hoped for reconciliation with Great Britain, and rumors that peace commissioners were being sent kept up their hopes. Meanwhile, the daily business of Congress dragged on. "Indians' affairs, revenue matters, naval arrangements and twenty other things," Adams wrote, "many of them very trivial, were mixed...with the great subjects of government, independence and commerce."

In April of 1776, Congress lifted the blockade of its own ports and set American commerce free, and in May it passed the long-delayed recommendation to the states to set up governments. Adams wrote a strong preamble to the recommendation, declaring that British authority "should be totally suppressed, and all the powers of government exerted under the authority of the people of the colonies." It was, of course, a statement of independence. The only thing needed now was a formal declaration.

This was proposed on June 7 by Richard Henry Lee and seconded by Adams. After three days of debate, the matter was postponed until July 1, and a committee consisting of Thomas Jefferson, John Adams, Benjamin Franklin, Roger Sherman, and Robert Livingston was appointed to draw up a declaration to the effect "that these United Colonies are, and of right ought to be, free and independent states."

The Declaration of Independence, written largely by Thomas Jefferson, with minor corrections by Franklin and Adams, was presented to the Congress on July 1, voted upon the next day, and formally approved on July 4, 1776. It was, of course, the most momentous event in the history of the colonies, for on that day the United States of America was born.

Chapter Five
Delegate and Diplomat (1776-1779)

Once the irrevocable step of independence had been taken, Congress turned to three matters of pressing importance: the prosecution of the war, a treaty to be proposed to France, and articles of confederation to be proposed to the states. John Adams served on two of the three committees that took up these issues.

"The committee to prepare a plan of treaties to be proposed to foreign powers" was appointed on June 12, 1776. Besides Adams, there was Dickinson, Franklin, Benjamin Harrison, and Robert Morris. It was left to Adams, however, to do most of the work of preparing the "Plan of Treaties."

His position was much the same as the one he had taken in Congress before the appointment, "that we should avoid all alliances which might embarrass us in after times and involve us in future European wars." He felt a commercial treaty "would be an ample compensation to France for acknowledging independence, and for furnishing us for our money or upon credit for a time with such supplies of necessaries as we should want, even if this conduct should involve her in a war."

The plan Adams drew up was submitted to Congress on July 18, ordered to be printed, and subsequently debated, amended, and adopted in its final form on September 17. Armed with copies of the plan, Benjamin Franklin, Silas Deane, and Thomas Jefferson were elected commissioners to the court of France on September 26, though Jefferson declined to serve and Arthur Lee replaced him. Securing the help of France was, of course, one of the most significant actions of Congress in winning the war of independence. The "Plan" Adams drew up served not only as the model for this treaty, but for all but one of the subsequent treaties entered into by America during the remainder of the century.

By far the most important committee Adams served on during his tenure in Congress, and the most burdensome to him, was the one called the Board of War and Ordnance. It was created on June 13 and Adams was made its chairman, a position which in effect made him Secretary of War for the United Colonies. The Board met every morning and evening, and all the routine military matters having to do with the prosecution of the war were referred to it. Among other duties, it was their responsibility to keep track of all officers, "artillery, arms, ammunition and warlike stores," and to "superintend the raising, fitting out, and dispatching all such land forces as may be ordered."

While Adams was busy as chairman of the Board, Congress continued to debate John Dickinson's proposed Articles of Confederation that would unite the colonies into a union. But here there were many difficult problems to be resolved. On what basis, for example, should each colony, or rather state, be represented? Should Congress have the authority to fix boundaries, to deal with the

Indians? How should the matter of slavery be handled? How should money be levied and appropriated? These and hundreds of other questions made it difficult to come to any agreement, and on August 20 the matter was postponed for later consideration.

Meanwhile, a communication was received from the British Admiral, Lord Howe, requesting a meeting with delegates from the Congress. There was no hint of what it might be about, but it could be a peace feeler, though Adams, especially, doubted it. Most in the Congress, however, felt it was at least worth finding out, and on September 6 Adams, along with Franklin and Edward Rutledge, was elected to a committee to confer with the Admiral, who had established headquarters in a house on Staten Island.

It was a dramatic episode that gained much attention. The committee left Philadelphia on September 9 and conferred with Howe on the 11th. Any hopes of peace any members of Congress might have held were soon dashed. "It did not appear," the committee reported to Congress on September 17, "that his Lordship's commission contained any other authority of importance than …that of granting pardons… and of declaring America, or any part of it, to be in the king's peace upon submission."

The committee of three was hardly back in Philadelphia when news reached Congress of the loss of New York City to the British. On August 27 Washington and his men had suffered a disastrous defeat on Long Island, barely escaping to Manhattan in small boats commanded by Colonel John Glover. With the British navy able to surround them, Manhattan proved to be indefensible.[2]

Washington withdrew his troops to Harlem Heights north of the city, where, the next day, September 16, they saw a contingent of British troops advancing northward along a valley in the terrain

2   *This episode is wonderfully treated in a small book by Bruce Bliven Jr. called* The Battle for Manhattan.

called the Hollow Way. To the surprise of the British, the Americans attacked, partially outflanking them, and killed many of them and wounded others. As they fled precipitately southward the Americans, flushed with success, could hardly be restrained.

For a time after that there was an uneasy truce. But by early October the British had moved ships up the Hudson as far as Tappan Zee, and up the East River and into Long Island Sound, ready to deploy troops. It became clear that they intended to surround the Americans, now located at Fort Washington, a mile north of Harlem Heights. To avoid entrapment, the Americans left their outpost, with 1,000 men to defend it, and retreated north, driven from one defensive position after another. Eventually they crossed the Hudson and began their long trek southward through New Jersey.

What disturbed Adams the most was news that the New Englanders had been the most precipitous in the flight. "The cowardice of New England men is an unexpected discovery to me," he wrote, "and I confess has put my philosophy to the trial." Another thing that disturbed him was the lack of discipline he had observed among the Continental troops. It was partly the news of the Manhattan debacle that spurred Congress to debate and approve the Articles of War on September 20.

Adams led the debate, paragraph by paragraph, upon these rules that were to govern the army for many years afterwards. Then, early in October, bone-weary and worn out from his exertions on behalf of Congress, he applied for and received permission for a leave of absence.

By the time Adams returned to Philadelphia, on February 1, 1777, the city had been threatened by the British, and Congress had removed itself to Baltimore. On December 8 of the year that had just ended, the last of Washington's troops crossed the Delaware as British troops appeared on the other side.

It was, as Thomas Paine was to write in the first of a series of essays published under the general rubric, *The Crisis,* "the winter of our discontent." The essay appeared on December 16 and had a great affect on the people. Paine was a powerful writer who achieved a huge readership with this and his previous pamphlets, *The Rights of Man* and *Common Sense,* and he did much to stir the American public to new resolve.

Instead of continuing the initiative, General Howe, accustomed to fighting only in fair weather, retired to New York for the winter, leaving three regiments of German Hessians at Trenton under the command of Lord Cornwallis. Many colonists, discouraged by the defeats, felt the war was lost. But then Washington began a series of brilliant maneuvers that restored the people's faith.

On Christmas night he crossed the Delaware with his troops and attacked the garrison at Trenton, inflicting a punishing blow before Cornwallis could counterattack. Evading Cornwallis' thrusts, on January 3, 1777, Washington and his troops met and defeated three regiments of British troops marching to the aid of Cornwallis. After that Cornwallis withdrew to New York, leaving New Jersey to the Americans. These victories stirred the nation to new resolves.

Congress, with the threat to Philadelphia removed, reconvened in that city early in March. Adams, meanwhile, had plunged into the work of the Board of War and Ordnance, which handled the bulk of Congress' routine matters, and was kept steadily busy throughout the spring and summer. Congress worked amidst persistent rumors that Howe was planning an attack on Philadelphia.

British reinforcements under the command of General Burgoyne were marching down from Canada, and the delegates were dismayed to learn that Fort Ticonderoga had fallen to them after only token resistance. Then, in May, General Howe began what looked like the start of his long-delayed campaign against Philadelphia when British troops marched out into the country.

The British were easily driven back by the Americans. After further delays, they boarded ships on July 23 and sailed to Chesapeake Bay, evidently intending to attack Philadelphia from the south. Washington drew up his forces on Brandywine Creek at Chad's Ford to check their advance. This time, however, the Americans were no match for the British, and they were decisively defeated on September 11, 1777.

The members of Congress, feeling there was still some chance Philadelphia might be saved, did not immediately evacuate the city. Then, at three o'clock in the morning, on Friday, September 19, Adams was awakened by James Lovell, one of his colleagues from Massachusetts, and "told that the members of Congress were gone, some of them, a little after midnight."

Lovell said they had a letter from Alexander Hamilton, who was Washington's Aide-de-camp, informing them "the enemy were in possession of the ford and the boats, and had it in their power to be in Philadelphia before morning...." They had, he wrote, "not a moment to lose" if Congress was to be removed.

With Congress and half the population gone, Philadelphia was occupied by the British troops on September 25. But as the members of Congress fled, first to Lancaster, then to York, not all the news was bad. The British General Burgoyne was in trouble, and had been ever since he had taken Fort Ticonderoga.

He continued his march toward Albany, but the loyalist support he had expected failed to materialize. A detachment of his troops under the command of General Barry Saint Leger was badly defeated at Oriskany in August and forced to withdraw to Canada. Despite that, Burgoyne pushed on.

The Continental army under General Gates was strongly entrenched at Bemis Heights, and in an attempt to move forward, Burgoyne suffered a defeat in what came to be called the first battle of Freeman's Farm. The date was September 19. On October 7 he was again defeated in a second battle at Freeman's Farm.

With his supplies almost gone, and virtually surrounded, Burgoyne surrendered to the Americans on October 17 at Saratoga. It was a decisive event, for this defeat was instrumental in bringing France into the war on the side of the Americans.

On November 7 Adams again applied for and received a leave of absence from Congress. He had every intention, he wrote later in his autobiography, of declining the next election and returning to his law practice. Four years of drudgery in Congress "and sacrifice of everything," he felt, was sufficient. Let another take his place. But he had no sooner returned to private practice while on leave when he received word that he had been appointed to the office of minister to France, along with Benjamin Franklin and Arthur Lee, replacing Silas Deane, who was being recalled.

He accepted the post out of a deep sense of responsibility, though it would mean a long separation from his family. There was also the very real danger of being captured on the high seas by the British and either spending the rest of the war in prison or being hanged for treason. "On the other hand," he wrote, "my country was in deep distress and in great danger. Her dearest interest would be involved in the relations she might form with foreign nations."

Adams had thought deeply upon the subject, and Congress was fully aware of his views. He could not decline. On February 13, 1778, taking his eldest son John Quincy with him, he bid his family a last farewell and boarded the 24-gun Continental frigate, the *Boston*, anchored off Hough's Neck in Quincy Bay. They got only as far as Marblehead, however, for gale winds and thick snow kept them from putting out to sea until the 17th.

Once clear of land, the *Boston* was immediately given chase by three British frigates, and they barely managed to elude capture after two days of sailing. Other than that, Adams wrote in his diary, life on board ship was "a dull scene." There was nothing to see but "sky, clouds and sea, and then sea, clouds and sky." He tried to brush up on his French and teach it to his ten-year-old Johnny, but with sea-sickness and damp, cramped quarters, little was accomplished.

Five weeks later they made land off the coast of Spain, near the port of St. Antonio, and headed north to Bordeaux. With alternate calm and opposing winds, it took them another week to make port. On Sunday, March 29, the day before they dropped anchor, a French pilot came on board and informed Adams that the French had declared war on the English four days before.

What had happened, as Adams was to learn later, was that France had signed treaties of alliance and commerce with the United States on February 6 at Versailles, and broken diplomatic relations with England on March 13. This was great news, indeed, and, though war was never formally declared, France was soon giving naval and other aid to the Americans.

In a sense, with the signing of these treaties, Adams' mission to France was over before it began. What remained were the more routine diplomatic matters: establishing the correct relations with France and soliciting the maximum help obtainable. But as a third member of the triumvirate, Adams felt like a fifth wheel.

Soon after his arrival in Paris he began writing to friends in Congress urging them to propose that the duties of minister to France be combined in one person, namely Franklin, who was doing a great job of personal diplomacy. It was, in effect, a request for his own recall. Congress, however, was not to act upon it until the following September. Meanwhile there was much work to do.

Diplomatic finances were in a mess, and the more routine work of the commission, such as correspondence, had been sadly neglected. Most distressing of all to Adams was the animosity that existed between the ministers. It had, he wrote, "divided all the Americans and all the French people connected with Americans or American affairs into parties very bitter against each other." Without taking sides, Adams worked assiduously to heal the breach, soothe ruffled tempers, and get the ministers together on a daily basis to discuss and plan diplomatic action. It was another reason, he felt, for having one man appointed with sole responsibility.

In the beginning, Adams found himself swept up in a swirl of social activities, meetings with the king, the ministers, and other notables of France, and every day in the week he received invitations to dine "in some great or small company." He soon determined to decline as many invitations as he could, to "attend to my studies of French and the examination and execution of that public business which suffered for want of our attention every day."

Devoting himself to the daily, routine matters that had been so neglected by Franklin and Lee, he gradually brought some order into the finances, handling the multitudinous details of the office and maintaining a voluminous correspondence. But as the months wore on, his thoughts turned increasingly to returning to Braintree and to Abigail and his family.

In October the first rumors reached him that he was to be recalled. There were, however, equally strong rumors that he was to be appointed minister to Holland. In February of 1779 official word finally reached Paris that Benjamin Franklin had been made sole minister plenipotentiary to France. Adams immediately made plans to return to America on board the frigate *Alliance*.

The *Alliance* was due to leave from Nantes in March. In this, however, Adams was to suffer what he called "a cruel disappointment." The departure was delayed from day to day, and at the end of April he was still in Nantes. Discouraged and depressed, he struck a melancholy note in his diary. "There is a feebleness and a langor in my nature," he wrote. "My mind and body both partake of this weakness. By my physical constitution, I am but an ordinary man. The times alone have destined me to fame – and even these have not been able to give me much."

Two days later, on the 28th, he received more bad news. The *Alliance* was not going to sail for some time and he was to take passage on the French frigate *Sensible*, leaving L'Orient in July. On the plus side, at L'Orient, he met and dined with Captain John Paul Jones, whom he characterized as "the most ambitious and intriguing officer in the American navy."

Jones had already received considerable notoriety for his raids on British shipping and an attack on the English seacoast. A few months later he was to achieve immortal fame for his attack on a large British convoy in the North Sea. He lashed his ship the *Bonhomme Richard* to the leading British ship, the heavily armed *Serepis,* and when called upon to surrender, replied, "I have not yet begun to fight." After three hours of hand-to-hand fighting aboard the vessels, he forced the British to surrender.

The *Sensible* finally left L'Orient on June 18 with Adams, John Quincy, and the new ambassador to the United States, the Chevalier de la Luzerne, aboard. A few days out at sea, Luzerne informed Adams that Spain was entering the war on the side of France, though without recognizing American independence. Other than that, the voyage, lasting little more than six weeks, was uneventful. The *Sensible* sailed into Boston Harbor on August 3, and Adams, with his son, was home in Braintree the same day.

After a joyful reunion, he immediately sat down to inform Congress of his return in a letter to its president, John Jay, following this up in a few days with a more detailed review of his commission and European affairs. These duties out of the way, he looked forward to a long period of calm and the pleasures of farm, family, and friends. As always, he was to be disappointed.

Home less than a week, he was elected by the town of Braintree to be their representative to the state convention scheduled to meet in September to draw up a new constitution for Massachusetts. Adams attended the first plenary session of this convention in Cambridge from September 1 through the 7th. On the 4th he was one of thirty members appointed to a committee to draft "a Declaration of Rights, and the form of a Constitution."

In actual fact, though, the writing of this draft devolved solely upon Adams, and he labored upon it, with frequent committee meetings, until the convention next met on October 28. At that time the completed document was presented for discussion, and was adopted by the convention in a third session early in 1780. It remains to this day, as amended, the basic law of Massachusetts.

Meanwhile, on September 27, Congress had again elected John Adams to high diplomatic office, this time as minister plenipotentiary to negotiate treaties of peace and commerce with Great Britain. Aware of "the high honor" of the appointment, he promptly accepted when official word reached him on November 3. Though the state constitutional convention was again in session, Adams immediately made plans to leave for France on the French frigate, the *Sensible*, anchored in Boston harbor.

Taking painful leave of his family on the 13th, he boarded the *Sensible* along with his two oldest boys, Charles, nine, and John Quincy, now twelve. Two days later, on November 15, 1779, the frigate put out to sea, carrying Adams on one of the most fateful, difficult, and important assignments of his long career.

Chapter Six
Minister Plenipotentiary (1780-1781)

It was a rough crossing. The ship was crowded with 350 sailors, plus passengers, and there was still the danger of being sunk or captured by British Men of War. This, as Adams later wrote in his autobiography, he considered the worst of evils. But they met none on this crossing; it was the weather that did them in.

Two days at sea Adams became aware the pumps were going and that the ship was taking on a great deal of water. The leak kept getting worse, and the pumps were worked day and night, till all on board, "passengers and officers as well as seamen, were almost exhausted with fatigue." Because of this, and the danger of sinking, the Captain decided to put in at the nearest landfall.

Sighting Cape Finisterre off the Spanish coast on Tuesday, December 7, he brought the ship into the Spanish port of El Ferrol the next day. It was a lively port, filled with a squadron of French warships. Though a stay there would not be dull, the delay for repairs caused Adams a dilemma. Should he travel by land to Paris, a journey he estimated at twelve or thirteen hundred miles, or wait for the frigate to be examined and repaired? Since it was estimated repairs might take four or five weeks, if indeed the ship was not condemned, Adams decided to make his way to Paris by land.

He hired two "muleteers" with the necessary wagons and servants to handle the food and luggage and to guide them. The next day he and his party rose early in the morning, Wednesday, December 15, and set out over the bad roads and high mountains to cross Spain. It was an arduous journey, with one of the muleteers leading their train of thirteen mules while the other followed to take care of the stragglers. They often had to climb the steep hills on foot, and the journey was made pestiferous by the fleas and bed bugs met with in the poor, smoke-filled rooms of the inns they stayed in at night.

Though treated with consideration and respect by officials, and with much warmth and hospitality by them and everyone else, they were distressed by the squalor and misery of the common people. On top of which there was the cold rain and snow of the Spanish winter. "All sick with violent colds and coughs," Adams wrote in his diary as they crossed the mountains of the Pyrenees in early January.

At last, fording the small stream that divided Spain from France, they entered the French village of St. John De Luz on January 20, 1780. Three days later they were in Bayonne. There they paid off their guides, purchased one post chaise, hired others, and the next day set off for Paris. Adams had had some fear of robbers because of the desolate countryside between Bayonne and Bordeaux, but there were none, and the journey was uneventful.

They arrived safely in Paris on February 9, in "tolerable health" as Adams wrote to Congress. The next morning he and Francis Dana, who was to be his aide, rode out to Passy where, after enrolling Adams' two boys in the school John Quincy had attended the year before, they spent the afternoon in conversation with Benjamin Franklin.

The next day Franklin accompanied them to Versailles and introduced them to the dignitaries, among them the Prime Minister de Maurepas, the Minister of Marine Sartine, and, most importantly, the Foreign Minister Comte de Vergennes. Adams, who had brief conversations with them all, was pleased with the cordiality of his reception.

"I never heard the French ministry so frank, explicit and decided... in their declarations to pursue the war with vigor and afford effectual aid to the United States," he wrote to the Congress on February 15. Most importantly, from his point of view, he was given permission to write to the Comte de Vergennes on the subject of his mission.

Though his mission to negotiate a treaty of peace with Great Britain was generally suspected, it was not specifically known, and he wrote in confidence. Vergennes, however, who had hoped Franklin might be appointed minister plenipotentiary, was wary. He wrote back that he saw "no inconvenience" if Adams were to speak of future "pacification," but warned him it would not be prudent to communicate his authority to negotiate a treaty of peace and commerce. He said it would be premature and might be seen as a sign of weakness.

Adams, eager to pursue his mission, was surprised and perplexed by this request. He saw it as an ingenious attempt on Vergennes' part to draw him out on his instructions, unaware that Vergennes, through the diligence of Gerard, his ambassador in America, knew quite well what his instructions were.

Years later, in his *Autobiography,* Adams depicted the delay as intrigue to get his commission to negotiate a treaty of commerce annulled so as "to keep us embroiled with England as much and as long as possible, even after a peace." But he wrote to Vergennes that he would conform to his advice and keep the intent of his mission quiet.

With so little to do publicly, Adams kept himself busy during the week writing letters, mostly to Congress (five long dispatches a week), and on weekends took his sons sightseeing. He also wrote articles for the newspapers that he hoped would further the American cause. Some of these, with Vergennes approval, appeared in the weekly *Mercure de France;* others, with the help of two Americans living in London, appeared anonymously in English newspapers.

During this period Adams' relationship with Vergennes went from bad to worse. For four months there was no correspondence at all. And when Vergennes did finally write, Adams responded with a series of impolitic letters critical of the French war effort. Vergennes, never happy with Adams, sent them to his ambassador in America, Gerard, with the suggestion he show them to members of Congress to encourage them to replace Adams with a single ambassador, the more agreeable, more diplomatic Franklin.

As spring gave way to summer, Adams found himself increasingly frustrated in his efforts to fulfill his mission. He cast about for something more he might do on the diplomatic front to further the American cause. Focusing his attention on The Netherlands, he traveled to Amsterdam in August with his two sons.

Though he had no official status, he knew that Henry Laurens, who had been appointed an envoy to The Netherlands, would be arriving soon, and he hoped to do some preliminary work to make his job easier. He also knew there was a possibility the Dutch, anxious for trade, might be persuaded to abandon their neutrality in favor of the Americans. He also hoped they might be willing to lend the Americans the money to purchase vital supplies.

What he didn't know was that Laurens, three weeks after leaving South Carolina in July to take up his duties, had been captured on the high seas by a British frigate and was now a prisoner of war who would be transferred to the Tower of London for the duration. It wasn't, in fact, until a month after taking up residence in Amsterdam that Adams heard of Laurens' capture.

The very next day, September 17, he received a dispatch from Congress informing him that the responsibility for dealing with the Dutch had been placed temporarily in his hands. It was a job, of course, that he took on with relish and considerable hope. He was convinced the time was ripe for not only the Dutch, but the other supposedly neutral nations of Europe, to establish commercial relations with the new nation despite the risks of war.

But his efforts, especially in the beginning, were stymied by his inability to speak or understand Dutch and by the fact that he had no entrée to the government (the Dutch, afraid of British reprisals, had not yet recognized the United States). Of much greater import, something Adams only gradually came to appreciate, were the complexities of the situation.

Catherine the Great of Russia, fearful of depredations on Russian shipping, had formed a League of Neutral Nations, which the Dutch had willingly joined, and a delicate balance was being maintained with the warring nations of Europe. Adding to his difficulties, he felt, was a lack of a true understanding of his country among the Dutch, and a gross overestimate of British power.

He concluded that a major informational and educational effort on his part was called for, which he began by publishing a copy of the recently-adopted Massachusetts constitution in the *Gazette de Leydon.* It was an important newspaper edited by one of his new-found Dutch friends, Jean Luzan, who subsequently published other articles Adams wrote or passed on to him.

Adams thought the task of educating the Dutch would be made easier by the many similarities between America and The Netherlands. The Netherlands, like The United States, had separated from their mother country, Spain, a century and a half before and set up an independent republic of seven provinces that had prospered mightily.

But the Dutch political system was more complicated. Though based on representative government and freedom, the executive power of The Netherlands, the Stadtholder, was weak, and the members of its legislature, the States-General, were beholden to the cities because the cities paid most of the taxes, and therefore had a major influence on the national government.

Bad news from America that fall also increased the difficulty of Adams' mission. The Dutch, always fearful of the British, were made increasingly apprehensive by news of American defeats. One of the worst was in Camden, South Carolina, where American forces under General Gates, one of America's best generals, had suffered a disastrous rout. And in November news reached them of the treason of General Benedict Arnold, who, after failing in an attempt to turn over the stronghold of West Point to the British, had defected to them.

Though the bad news made the future of the new nation seem dim, Adams himself was not one to be discouraged for long. He renewed his efforts to achieve a commercial treaty with the Dutch and to secure the loan and supplies so vitally needed for the American war effort. Five months after arriving in Amsterdam he had still not been granted an interview with a single government official. What he did instead was to work hard at establishing relationships with those sympathetic to the American cause, especially people in commerce and banking and the media.

Then two things happened that encouraged him in his efforts. In late December the British recalled Richard Yorke, their ambassador to The Hague, and began an unofficial war against Dutch shipping. In late February Adams learned he had been made minister plenipotentiary to The Netherlands, with all the rights and responsibilities it implied to conduct the business of the Congress and conclude treaties of commerce with the Dutch.

The title, however, gave him no greater access to government officials than before. The Dutch still did not recognize the new nation, and diplomatic protocol dictated that any ambassador newly appointed to a country must wait for an indication of that nation's willingness to receive him before applying for recognition at The Hague.

Frustrated, Adams set out to tour the seven provinces of The Netherlands to get a sense of how the people regarded the United States vis-à-vis Great Britain, and how they viewed the war for independence. What he found was a nation divided in their opinions. With Britain raiding their shipping, some were all for being firm and resolute; others, afraid of war, were against even appearing to side with the United States.

He was convinced, however, that in time not only the Dutch, but the neutral nations, because of the British raids and because their commercial interests would benefit greatly from trade with the new country, would come out on the side of the United States. All it would require, he felt, was a much greater effort on his part to bring them around to that point of view.

Having been advised that his living quarters were not fit for an ambassador to entertain in, or otherwise build and maintain relationships with important Dutch contacts, he set about securing a proper house. It would, of course, have to include servants and livery and fine furnishing so he might wine and dine and properly impress the people whose interest and sympathies were vital in winning the government over to the American cause.

As was usual with him, he also turned to the pen and to publication, and that spring wrote many letters and articles he hoped would win over the people and influence the course of events. In addition, he worked on a long, sixteen-page "memorial" he intended to present to the States-General if the present stalemate continued. The memorial reviewed the history of the relationship between the peoples of their two countries, the history of the present conflict with Great Britain, and, outlining his mission as minister plenipotentiary, presented his credentials.

It was an unheard of thing to do, very much against protocol, and it could have put his entire mission at risk and cost him his job. Nevertheless, he had it translated into Dutch and, against the advice of many, especially the French, set out for The Hague, the seat of the Dutch government, on April 19, 1781 (the sixth anniversary of the start of the War for Independence), to present it to the States-General. The only concession he made to the French was to first visit their ambassador at The Hague, the Duc de La Vauguyon, to consult with him and show him the document. La Vauguyon, however, was not able to dissuade Adams from taking what the French considered a rash and foolish step.

Adams called first on the Grand Pensionary of the States-General, Pieter Van Bleiswyck, who politely refused to accept the memorial. He said it would first have to be presented to the president of the States-General, who might then present it to the whole body of the legislature. Adams duly called on the president at The Hague, who that week happened to be the Baron Lynden van Hemmen (the Dutch rotated the assignment), on May 4, 1781. The president also refused to accept the document.

When Adams replied that the Baron's refusal left him with no choice but to publish the memorial so the Dutch people and all the world might know of his mission, the Baron smiled and said that then he, the Baron, might be able to present it to the members of the States-General as a published document, an act which in no way implied his endorsement.

Adams therefore had the memorial published in Dutch, French, and English, in newspapers in The Netherlands and France. It subsequently appeared in newspapers throughout Europe, and created a huge stir. Though the response of the Dutch people was favorable, it had no effect whatsoever on the Dutch government as far as encouraging their recognition of the United States, and their recognition of Adams as its emissary.

The excitement occasioned by its publication had hardly subsided when news of a peace mediation effort by Russia stirred the governments and peoples of Europe. A congress of the concerned nations was to meet in Vienna in July to discuss a peace effort that proposed a cease fire between the colonies and Great Britain for a full year while they attempted to settle their differences. Vergennes, anxious to consult with Adams, quickly summoned him to Paris.

From Adams' point of view there were a number of things seriously wrong with the proposal that made him reluctant to engage himself in the discussion. First, all forces were to remain in place, which meant Great Britain would continue to occupy the cities of New York, Charleston, and Savannah, the state of Maine, and large tracts of land in other areas. Second, the proposal used the term "the colonies," making it clear there was to be no recognition of its nationhood prior to any settlement.

To Adams this was absolutely unacceptable: Recognition *must* precede peace. What was worse, Congress was not invited to send a participant to the Vienna congress, only a representative, which meant, as Adams had feared, that France was to act as proxy for "the colonies." Much to his relief, Great Britain refused to participate in the congress, and the peace effort came to naught.

Shortly after returning to Amsterdam, Adams fell ill with a malaria-type illness, induced possibly by stress and his normal capacity for overwork. The illness kept him from useful work for more than six weeks, during which time Congress, at the urging of Luzerne, the new French ambassador, decided to appoint a ministry of five men, rather than just one, to represent the varied interests of the united colonies. The five men appointed were Laurens from South Carolina, Jefferson from Virginia, John Jay from New York, Franklin from Philadelphia, and Adams from New England.

Since Laurens was still imprisoned, Jay declined to serve, and Jefferson was reluctant to leave Virginia, this left Franklin and Adams to continue the business of war and peace overseas. The big difference now was that Adam's responsibility as sole minister plenipotentiary for peace was, in his view, severely restricted.

In some respects he may have thought it a good thing, for he wrote to Franklin, who had sent the news on from Paris, that "Congress may have done very well to join others in the commission for peace." On the other hand, he may have been feeling the onset of the illness that would incapacitate him, or was simply putting a positive spin on the decision. For at the time he also wrote to a friend, James Searle, saying he felt he had been "fleeced."

In any event it must have been a severe blow to his pride and could only have added to the pressures that contributed to the illness to which he was succumbing. He afterwards referred to the illness as a "nervous fever." But whatever it was, it laid him so low he was out of his mind for five days at one point, unable to work, and hardly aware of where he was. It wasn't until mid-October that he began his slow recovery and was able again to work.

Toward the end of November, news reached The Netherlands from America of an event that was to change the course of the war and the peace effort, and make it possible for Adams to finally obtain from the Dutch the money so desperately needed by America to pay its soldiers and purchase the supplies for a war effort that had been going on now for more than six years.

The news was that Cornwallis, the British general, had been defeated at Yorktown and taken prisoner with more than seven thousand of his men. It came about as the result of something Adams had long been urging the French to do: use its fleet to engage the British men-of-war. He had since the beginning been a strong advocate of sea power, and had been instrumental in establishing what was at least the beginnings of a U.S. Navy shortly after their declaration of independence. It was his belief that the war could not be won without the use of naval forces.

Now at last it had happened. Cornwallis, preparing for an attack on Philadelphia, where the Congress was sitting, had moved the major share of his forces to a strip of land in Virginia along Chesapeake Bay called Yorktown. At this point Washington received word at long last that Admiral de Grasse was moving his fleet north from the West Indies to blockade the Chesapeake.

He immediately marched his army, with the French troops under Rochambeau, from New York to engage the British army, which would be effectively bottled up by the French fleet and unable obtain help or relief from its own navy. The result, on October 19, 1781, was a stunning victory for the Americans and the French.

The surrender of Cornwallis with 7,241 of his men was a terrible defeat for the British, whose treasury and morale had long been sapped by what seemed like an interminable war. There was no way they were going to be able to replace almost eight thousand of their best-trained soldiers, or find the will and money required to continue the fighting. Though a peace treaty would not be signed for another two years, the American war for independence was in effect over. When Adams received the news, he immediately renewed his efforts to secure the much-needed loan the United States so desperately needed to conclude the conflict and establish itself as a viable nation.

Chapter Seven
Diplomat and Ambassador
(1782-1788)

When the "glorious news," as Adams called it, of Cornwallis' defeat reached Amsterdam on the night of November 23, he immediately resolved to renew his efforts. His first goal was to be recognized by the Dutch government, his second to obtain the loan so desperately needed by the United States to pay for its war effort.

This time, however, it was with the approval of the French ambassador to The Hague, the Duc de la Vauguyon. By the middle of December the Duke had come to agree that, in light of the British debacle at Yorktown, it was perhaps time for Adams to "demand" to be permitted to present his credentials to the Dutch government at The Hague..

On January 8, 1782, Adams called on the President of the States-General. He was turned away. He next called on the Grand Pensionary, but the Grand Pensionary pleaded illness. Twice rebuffed, Adams decided to take his case to the people by calling on the representatives of the provinces at their houses in The Hague.

He began by calling first on the Pensionary of Dort. After that, he called at the house of Leyden, then continued with the others. Everywhere, he writes, he met with an "affectionate and friendly reception," but each said they could do nothing. At last, calling at the house of Friesland, he was told the Frieslanders were resolved to recognize his new nation.

If the Frieslanders vote for recognition, the burgomaster of Amsterdam assured him, the other provinces would soon follow suit. Adams was not so sanguine, but the burgomaster turned out to be right. On February 26, 1782, the province of Friesland voted to urge the States-General to formally recognize Adams as the United States representative.

After that the citizens of Leyden submitted a petition urging recognition of the United States, and other cities soon followed. But it wasn't until the provinces of Holland and West Friesland, two of The Netherland's most important provinces, submitted petitions urging that Adams be accepted as ambassador of the United States that he knew recognition was assured.

Meanwhile, there was a peace feeler to be considered. Thomas Digges, an American living in London, called on Adams in Amsterdam with a query as to whom should be contacted in the event Great Britain sought peace. Aware this might only be a straw in the wind, Adams responded cautiously. He told Digges there were other commissioners beside himself who would have to be contacted in the event a formal offer was made, and advised him to contact Franklin and de Vergennes in Paris.

On April 19, 1782, seven years to the day after the musket shot that began the Revolution had been fired on the commons at Lexington,

Adams received at last the long coveted recognition he had sought so arduously: The States-General of the United Provinces resolved he be accepted as envoy of the United States of America and granted an audience "when he shall demand it."

It was *pro forma*, and an audience with the Prince of Orange soon followed. Adams found the audience with the Prince most cordial and pleasant. In the ensuing weeks there were calls to be made, and received, on the many government officials who wanted to congratulate him and make his acquaintance. The Duc de la Vauguyon even threw him an embassy ball at which he was the center of attention, and where the Spanish ambassador commended him on "the great blow" he had struck for freedom.

Now that he was officially minister plenipotentiary, Adams took up residence in The Hague in May in an opulently furnished building he called the "United States House." He then turned his efforts toward his second goal, that of obtaining a loan to pay the costs of, and to continue, the war with Britain. For though Britain had suffered a disastrous defeat, there was still no assurance that a peace treaty would be signed.

Obtaining a loan, it turned out, was much easier than expected. Because of his success in obtaining recognition, Adams was besieged by offers from banking houses desiring to attempt to negotiate a loan. None, however, were willing to guarantee such a loan, and he turned finally to a consortium of bankers willing to guarantee a loan at four and a half per cent. The initial agreement, signed on June 11, 1782, was for $2,000,000, though Adams eventually managed to increase this to $4,000,000.

It wasn't the $10,000,000 the Congress needed, but it was, for the times, an immense sum, and obtaining this loan was an achievement of which Adams was quite justifiably proud. In fact, he considered it his greatest contribution to the cause of American independence. "If this had been the only action of my life," he wrote Abigail, "it would have been well spent." Many historians agree, for it was crucial to the success of the new nation in its fight for freedom. It also added pressure on Britain to recognize the colonies as a new nation and to conclude a peace.

During this period Adams learned that Lord North, who had been British Prime Minister for twelve years and was opposed to American independence, had resigned on March 20. It seemed likely that persons more favorable to the American cause would come to power, chief among them Charles James Fox, who had opposed Lord North in Parliament and favored American independence, and Lord Shelburne, who also favored the colonies.

Fox, however, was unacceptable to the King, and Shelburne, who *was* acceptable, was unable to form a ministry. As a result, the task of forming a new government fell upon a former Prime Minster, Lord Rockingham, who at least had the virtue, from the American point of view, of having had the Stamp Act repealed under his previous ministry. But what actions he might take were unknown.

The months of political in-fighting among the candidates had left peace negotiations up in the air. Though Fox and Shelburne, long-time rivals, had each sent out separate peace feelers, Fox to Vergennes and Franklin, Shelburne to Franklin alone, their efforts were fruitless, since neither had been able to gain power. Then, on July 1, 1782, Rockingham died unexpectedly and Shelburne was named Prime Minister.

As Prime Minister, Shelburne took all the powers of the peace negotiations into his own hands. And the fact that the agent he had sent previously to discuss peace, a Scottish merchant named Richard Oswald, had called on Franklin but not Vergennes set the pattern for the Americans to proceed independently of the French. Franklin saw the advantage to the United States in doing this and did not inform Vergennes of the negotiations, which he began with the help of John Jay, the American ambassador to Spain, who joined him in Paris.

In late September, Jay sent Adams, the third American negotiator, an urgent message that he come to Paris "soon – very soon." Adams, busy negotiating the treaty of commerce with the Dutch, was reluctant to leave. He was obviously unaware of how close they were to a peace treaty. It is also evident he was not anxious to rejoin Franklin, whom he had come to dislike, nor to become involved again in the intrigues of France. Even after the Dutch treaty was signed at the State House in The Hague, on October 8, it took him more than a week to hire a coach and set off for Paris, which included sightseeing on the way.

When he arrived, Jay, who had been conducting the discussions with Oswald most of the summer (Franklin, ill with gout and bladder stones, had missed most of them), filled him in on what had so far taken place. Jay said he had insisted that no peace could be negotiated until Britain first recognized the colonies as an independent nation. That, he told Adams, was why he had waited until Oswald received word from Britain that he had the authority to conclude a peace with the "ministers of the United States of America" before sending for him.

Adams, of course, agreed with his decision, and was elated at the prospect of peace. The only fly in the ointment was a Congressional directive from Robert Livingston informing them that in seeking peace they should be guided by the French. Outraged, Adams wrote an angry letter to Livingston. In the end, after much discussion among themselves, the three ministers decided to ignore the directive and proceed without consulting the French. It was a bold move, but one that promised to be of much benefit to the United States, since they wouldn't have Vergennes intervening with French concerns.

Formal discussions began with the British negotiators on October 30 in Jay's residence at the Hotel d'Orleans and continued for the next six days. Several tentative agreements were reached, but since the British delegation could not enter into formal agreements without the approval of their government, they sent Henry Strachey, one of the members of their delegation, to London to secure it. When he returned, on November 25, final negotiations began and continued through the end of the month.

By then only two major obstacles remained: American fishing rights in the North Atlantic, about which Adams was adamant, and the compensation America was to pay the Loyalists who had had their property seized. Adams managed to secure the first, but Franklin and Jay felt strongly that no compensation should be paid. There was much bickering, but in the end they agreed to the inclusion of a statement in the treaty that Congress would "earnestly recommend" each state to provide compensation.

On November 30 the American and British delegates signed a preliminary treaty to go into effect when ratified by their respective governments, and when the hostilities between the European nations should cease. It was a triumph for the United States and its three negotiators – Jay, Franklin, and Adams.

Even Vergennes admitted he had not conceived the war could have been concluded on such generous terms. He called Adams "the Washington of diplomacy." But, obviously irritated at being left out of the negotiations, wrote to a colleague that he thought the British had "bought" the peace by making too many concessions.[3]

---

3   *Noted American historian Gordon S. Wood, author of* The American Revolution, *has called this treaty "the greatest achievement in the history of American diplomacy."*

In America there were heated debates in Congress about the ministers' failure to obey their order to follow Vergennes' lead, but the terms of the treaty were generous enough to eventually quiet the criticism. It only remained now for Franklin to apologize to Vergennes for not keeping him informed of the negotiations (which he did most tactfully, even securing more money from the French), and for the hostilities between the three European powers to come to an end.

The hostilities between France, Spain, and Britain came to a quick conclusion now that the British and Americans had made their peace, and the final articles of "peace and armistice" were signed in January of 1783, with all parties to the hostilities present. Copies were sent to the countries involved for formal approval by their governments. After more than eight years of war, the definitive treaty was signed in Paris September 3.

Adams, who had been apart from Abigail for more than three years (he had resigned his commission earlier in the year but agreed to stay on until Congress released him), now began to think of home. However, a rumor that an ambassador was to be appointed to the Court of St. James, something Adams had strenuously urged on Congress, made him reluctant to leave.

The truth was, despite the exchange of letters between himself and Abigail expressing their longings to be together, it was a post he very much wanted. Also, about this time, the illness with its strange, flu-like symptoms that had plagued him two years earlier recurred. He was seriously ill for only a few days this time. But before he had fully recovered, word arrived from America that he had been appointed to head a commission, which included Jefferson and Franklin, to negotiate treaties of commerce with Britain and the other nations of Europe.

Abigail, increasingly frustrated by her husband's unwillingness to return home, became determined to join him in Europe. Adams, who had previously wavered, finally agreed. He, of course, had no idea when or where she would arrive, or, for that matter, when Jefferson would arrive so the work of the commission could begin. With time on his hands, he decided to go to Bath, England, where the waters were said to be salutary, to recover further from his illness.

Arriving in London on October 26, he was so taken with this city of 750,000 inhabitants, which reminded him of his own country, that he lingered for two months, meeting friends and visiting the sights he had only read about. Finally he set out for Bath, where he arrived on December 24. But he hardly had time to benefit from the curative waters when word reached him of difficulties with the Dutch over America's reluctance to pay its debt.

Since all his work with the Dutch would have been in vain, and the commercial credit of his new country ruined, if something was not done about it immediately, he cut short his vacation and hurried to The Netherlands. There, after securing a new loan to repay the old, though at what was considered an exorbitant interest of six per cent, he found he was reluctant to return to Paris.

He still had no idea of when or where Abigail would arrive, and decided to wait for her in The Netherlands. By now spring had arrived and, unbeknownst to him, Abigail, who had written her last letter on May 25, 1784, had set sail for England on June 20 with their daughter Nabby and two servants on the merchant ship *Active*. The voyage was largely uneventful, except for a storm off the Grand Banks. But when they reached the English Channel, gale winds made it impossible for them to sail up the Thames.

As a result, they were taken from the ship by a small boat and put ashore at Deal, on the southern coast of England, seventy miles from

London. The next morning, hiring a post chaise, they set off for the capitol. By nightfall they were ensconced in rooms in the Adelphi, a hotel not far from the Thames where Adams had previously stayed. Abigail immediately sat down and wrote a letter addressed to Adams at The Hague.

Adams responded that her letter informing him that she and Nabby were in London had made him "the happiest man on earth." But, unfortunately, unfinished business negotiating new loans with the Dutch prevented him from leaving immediately. He sent the letter via their son John Quincy, now a tall young man of seventeen who had recently returned from Russia where he had been secretary to Dana. The letter instructed his family to wait for him at the hotel. John Quincy arrived at the hotel on July 30, pleasantly surprising his mother and sister. John arrived a week later, on August 7. It was, however, a short, if happy, reunion.

Adams received word that Jefferson had landed in France and was on his way to Paris to join him and Franklin on the commission to negotiate treaties of commerce. He and his family set off early the next morning for Paris where, after a few days of shopping and sightseeing, they rented the "enormous house" at Auteuil that Adams had occupied the year before. It was a mansion of fifty rooms, four miles outside the city, with a view of the Seine and situated next to the park, the Bois de Boulogne, where Adams frequently went for walks. More importantly, it was only a mile from Franklin at Passy, where the commission would meet to conduct business.

The work of the commission was arduous and difficult, but the trio worked well together. Adams and his family even got along well with Franklin and formed close bonds with Jefferson, who frequently entertained Abigail and the children in Paris. The work of the commission, however, was largely a failure. Of the twenty European nations only Prussia, in the end, signed a treaty of commerce with the United States. Britain, the nation with which a treaty of commerce was most wanted, refused to negotiate a commercial treaty until the United States appointed an ambassador.

Congress, afraid of European entanglements, was reluctant to do this. Finally, at the end of April 1785, Jefferson brought Adams word that he had been appointed Ambassador to the Court of St. James, and was expected to report for his new duties no later than June 4. This left John and Abigail only three weeks for packing and saying their goodbyes. They sent John Quincy back to America where, on November 20, he would enter the junior class at Harvard. Four days later, on May 20, 1785, John, Abigail, and Nabby set out for the port of Calais and the trip across the choppy waters of the English Channel.

Arriving in London the next day, they found most of the hotels, including the Adelphi, full. It was the King's birthday, and celebrations, including royal festivities with music by Handel, had brought many people in from outlying districts into the city. The Adamses managed to secure temporary quarters in the Bath Hotel in Piccadilly, the noisy heart of London.

Adams immediately notified the Secretary of State for Foreign Affairs for Great Britain, Lord Carmarthen, of his arrival, and Carmarthen invited Adams by return messenger to call on him the next day at either his office or residence. Adams chose Carmarthen's residence in Grosvenor Square, where he was "promptly and politely received." Following protocol, he showed Carmarthen his commission and requested that he might be presented to the King.

Carmarthen arranged for him to call on the king on June 1, when Carmarthen himself would present Adams "in closet," meaning privately. It was an historic occasion. The two old arch-enemies,

King George III and the rebel Yankee, were civil and polite. Adams, dressed in new clothes and wearing a sword, made an appropriately flowery speech and was accepted as ambassador from the new nation. Afterwards, speaking informally, the King, who liked to talk, said, "There is an opinion among some people that you are not the most attached of all your countrymen to the manners of France." Temporarily disconcerted, Adams replied diplomatically, "I must avow to Your Majesty I have no attachment but to my own country."

Three weeks later, as required by custom, Abigail and Nabby were also presented at court, this time to Queen Charlotte as well as the King. It was a long ceremony lasting several hours, at which the King and Queen slowly made their way in opposite directions around a large circle of guests. To Abigail the Queen seemed fatigued and uncomfortable, the King "jovial and good-humored." When he asked her, making small talk, if she loved walking, she replied, "No, I fear I am rather indolent in that respect." He bowed and moved on.

After the excitement of the ceremony was over, the Adamses turned to finding themselves a suitable house that would also serve as the legation of the United States. The house they found was at Number 8, Grosvenor Square, where not only Lord Carmarthen but other embassies were located. It was ideally located, on a quiet, tree-lined street, apart from the bustle of the city proper, yet set among the other embassies where John would be doing much of his work.

In the beginning, aside from the normal duties of running an embassy, such as dealing with the many expatriates and other Americans in London who called on him for one reason or another, by far the most important problem Adams faced was obtaining a commercial treaty between his country and Britain.

He worked most diligently at this, but soon came to the realization that his chances of success were minimal. The British treated him with "cold civility," and the anti-American feeling Adams quickly sensed was pervasive. His first objective, to open British ports to American shipping, was made even more difficult by Congress' refusal to take retaliatory action against British shipping to America, something Adams strongly urged but Congress was reluctant to do.

Adams also made little progress with Lord Carmarthen, who listened politely to what he had to say, but in the end took no steps that would help him achieve his goals. The King's position, as it was explained to him, was that the British would fulfill their part of the bargain (i.e., vacate their military posts on the frontier) when the United States fulfilled its part (i.e., compensate British citizens for loss of their property in America). But the United States, deep in debt because of the war, did not have the money to recompense the British, and so any progress was at a standstill.

Despairing of achieving any commercial or political accords, Adams thought longingly of returning to America. In early 1787 he sent a request to Congress to replace him with someone else. At this point in time it seemed hardly likely. What made the situation even more distressing was news from the States indicating that civil unrest and factionalism were taking place in, of all places, Massachusetts.

In the autumn of 1786 a group of farmers in Massachusetts, led by a former captain in the Continental army named Daniel Shay, had risen in revolt against what they felt was the unfair collection of debts and foreclosures on their farms. Some saw in the rebellion, before it was put down by the Massachusetts army, the beginning of anarchy and class warfare. The simple truth was, the nation had yet to form a government strong enough to deal effectively with the problems faced by thirteen disparate states.

There had been, for example, no issue of federal paper money backed by gold. This is what the rebel farmers were calling for in place of the various paper monies in circulation that were often not honored at face value. In fact, it was the lack of a "sound currency" that had caused the many hardships the farmers were suffering. The worthless currency made it impossible for them, and the working poor, to pay the excessive poll and land taxes they were forced to pay. On top of which, the country had fallen into a serious depression.

Adams at that time was working on the first volume of his three-volume *A Defence of the Constitutions of Government of the United States*. It was a defense of a tripartite government consisting of a strong executive, a separate judiciary, and a bicameral legislature, something he had long felt strongly about. He meant it to be read not only by Europeans but by his own countrymen, who would soon be meeting in Philadelphia to form a federal government. He hoped it would be based on the principles he was advocating, and copies did, indeed, arrive in time to influence the delegates gathering for the convention.

The news of Shay's Rebellion, as it came to be known, was deeply disturbing to him. He called it "extremely pernicious." Though he wrote to Jefferson in Paris that "all will be well," it perhaps added to his desire to return to the States. There he thought he might more effectively support his country in this critical phase it was going through, which would include, of course, the creation of a federal constitution to strengthen the Articles of Confederation.

To this end a Constitutional Convention was convened at the State House (now known as Independence Hall) in Philadelphia on May 25, 1787. It was chaired by George Washington, and the 55 delegates who attended represented all of the States except Rhode Island, which declined to send delegates. Almost immediately the idea of strengthening the Articles was scrapped, and the delegates set out to write a new Federal Constitution for these United States of America.

Remarkably, a written constitution was achieved in only a few short months, and by September the convention was able to adjourn. Though some thought of it as a "bundle of compromises," the constitution they agreed upon proved to be of enduring consequence. Adams had reason to be pleased. Not only did it provide for a tripartite government, but it gave extensive powers to the federal government. This included the power to levy and collect taxes, to borrow money, establish uniform duties and taxes, coin money, regulated interstate commerce, raise an army and navy, and grant patents and copyrights – in short, to function largely as the federal government does today.

After the delegates dispersed, all that remained for the document they had drafted to go into effect was for it to be ratified by at least nine of the thirteen states. There was much spirited discussion in most of the states. Virginia would only sign if it were decided to add a Bill of Rights. This was readily agreed to, and the first state, Delaware, ratified the Constitution in December. The others soon followed. Two states, North Carolina and Rhode Island, that had initially rejected the document, changed their minds after the Constitution was approved by all the other states.

In the spring of 1788, a year after Adams made his request to Congress to be replaced as Ambassador to Britain, he was finally relieved of his duties. It had been a busy year. In addition to handling the everyday concerns of the embassy and working on the Defence, which was finally published in three volumes, he managed, with the help of Jefferson, to conclude treaties of commerce with Portugal and Tripoli, and to renew the Dutch loans.

His last trip to The Netherlands for this purpose was a hurried one in March, where he was assisted by Jefferson. On his return to England he barely had time for the ceremonial farewells required of him before, in April, he and Abigail set sail, at long last, for home. What awaited him when he reached America he had scant idea. All his longing for the moment was to see his beloved Braintree once again and to be with the young children that neither he nor Abigail had seen for many long years

Chapter Eight
Vice-President Adams (1789-1796)

It was not a quiet home-coming. John Adams and Abigail had expected to slip in quietly to Massachusetts and their home. Instead, they were truly surprised by the reception that awaited them as their ship, the *Lucretia*, sailed into Boston Harbor. The fort in the bay called The Castle, alerted by a signal from the lighthouse ten miles beyond Boston, fired its cannons in a deafening salute as the ship passed, and John Hancock, now Governor, had his carriage meet John and Abigail at the wharf and return with them to his mansion.

He invited them to "tarry till you have fixed upon your place of abode." But Adams knew quite well where his abode was to be – the new house they had purchased in Braintree and which they were anxious to see. Hancock wanted to escort them there in style and had made arrangements for the town of Braintree to turn out to welcome them. But Adams, made uneasy by all the attention, skipped out and rode alone on horseback to the home of Abigail's sister Mary Cranch in Milton, where he was joined shortly afterwards by Abigail.

There they would stay until their furniture was unloaded and the new house ready to receive them. Abigail went over there the next day, and was dismayed by all the work still to be done to get it ready for them. But there was no holding John back. Eager to settle down once again as a farmer and lawyer, or so he liked to think, he ordered cattle for which they had no barn and spent the first few days roaming the land, making himself familiar with every nook and cranny, every tree and crag, of the 68 acres, even viewing with nostalgia the bay and their old house in Braintree from a hilltop.

Adams was fooling no one but himself. He had no real intention of settling down to the practice of law and farming. Though he was elected and declined to be a representative to Congress, and had no wish to be a senator or judge, he had other ambitions. The politics of the time held that one should not express one's desire for high office, but Adams dearly wanted high office in the new administration about to be elected that fall. While he couldn't expect to be the first President of the new United States (it was generally agreed that office would go to Washington), he decided he would have no other office but that of the Vice-President.

Meanwhile Nabby, now in New York with her husband Colonel William Smith, was expecting her second baby, and Abigail was determined to be there to help her daughter in her birth and confinement. This would leave her husband on his own, but he would hardly be alone. Old friends and relatives came constantly calling, and for a time he had with him his three sons. John Quincy came from Newburyport, where he was "reading the law," to stay while Abigail was away, and Charles, eighteen, and Thomas Boylston, fifteen, visited from Harvard where they were students.

Abigail arrived in New York too late to be there for the birth of their grandson, which his parents named John Adams Smith, but she stayed some months to help Nabby and to be with the child. She wrote to her husband that she hoped to be back in Braintree by Christmas, and sent word that Colonel Smith had seen a letter Alexander Hamilton had written James Madison stating that Adams "will certainly have all our votes and interest for Vice-President." This seemed an assurance that Adams would indeed be nominated for, and attain, that position.

Early in March, shortly after the electors cast their ballots in February, Adams received unofficial word he had been elected Vice-President. Official word would have to wait until Congress convened and the ballots of the electors were counted. This occurred on April 6, when the votes were opened and recorded by the President of the Senate. Despite some shenanigans by Hamilton to ensure Adams did not get too many votes, the final tally was 69 for Washington and 34 for Adams. According to the rules first laid down in the Constitution, this meant Washington had been elected President and Adams was to be Vice-President.

It should have been happy news for Adams, but, unaware of Hamilton's intrigues to reduce the vote for him, he was furious that he had received only half the number of votes cast for Washington. He thought of spurning the post. He wrote his friend Benjamin Rush that only the thought of the "great mischief" his refusal to accept the post might do, and its possible contribution to the "final failure" of the government, kept him from rejecting it.

As was often the case with Adams, his bark was worse than his bite. When the official news of his election reached Braintree on April 12, he was ready and waiting, his bags packed. He left the next day for Boston accompanied by a troop of light horse, leaving Abigail, still exhausted from her trip to New York, temporarily behind. In Boston the church bells rang and he was feted at the Governor's mansion by

John Hancock and served a lunch at which the local dignitaries had gathered to wish him well.

After lunch his small party set off for New York. They were greeted in every town through which they passed by waving and enthusiastic villagers. At Hartford Adams was presented with a new coat of local manufacture, and in New Haven he received the freedom of the city. When he crossed the state line into New York, he was met by the Westchester Light Horse and escorted to the northern tip of Manhattan. There he was met by an official reception committee that accompanied him to the house of John Jay in lower Manhattan.

Washington hadn't arrived yet, but Adams was sworn in as Vice-President and addressed the Senate. His speech was warmly applauded, after which he took his seat as chair of the Senate. The first order of business was determining the proper protocol for sending and receiving messages to and from the House of Representatives. At first it was agreed that any such intercourse should include ritual bows, but the House, in committee, rejected this, and the Senate acquiesced. When this first order of business was concluded, the first session of the Senate was adjourned to wait the arrival of Washington.

Washington reached the Hudson on April 23 and was ferried across to Manhattan on a large barge manned by thirteen pilots. The barge was filled with dignitaries, including the Governor of New York, members of both houses of Congress, and key officers of the government. The river was filled with boats of every description, and repeated volleys filled the air as his barge made its way across the river to Manhattan. There Washington was met by a welcoming committee that included many of his old officers, and that evening there was a state dinner. The next day Adams called to pay his respects.

The inauguration took place on April 30 before an assembled Congress. Adams met Washington at the door, conducted him to a special chair, and after a brief, if awkward speech, indicated it was time for Washington to take the oath of office. This was administered by Chancellor Livingston, Chief Justice of the New York judiciary. It was followed by three cheers, and the President then delivered his inaugural speech. When it was concluded, Congress adjourned and walked to near-by St. Paul's Church for prayers.

When Congress reconvened, the first order of business was to decide how the President should be addressed. In the House of Representatives it was agreed Washington should be addressed as simply President of the United States. But in the Senate, for a whole month, there was wrangling over the subject of titles. Much of it was occasioned by Adams' insistence upon some more honorific title than merely "Mr. President." It was more than a debate about titles, however. It was the beginning of the great debate, which has extended into our own times, between a strong executive and a strong legislature. It was the beginning of the formation of political parties, something Adams was very much against since he felt it would contribute to rancor and divisiveness.

But he felt so passionately the need for a strong executive and a strong federal government that he could not stop himself from joining in the debate. At one point, against the rules as they had yet to be established and to the dismay of many of the Senators, he lectured them for forty minutes. As a result, he earned a few enemies and the reputation for being a monarchist, meaning someone who wanted the Presidency to be for life and perhaps hereditary. Someone even suggested that flubsy Adams, short and stouter than ever, should be called "His Rotundity," a witticism that made it into the newspapers.

Despite their disagreements, Congress adjourned at the end of September after a remarkably productive first session. While it failed to pass a tariff bill (here it was more a disagreement between the rural majority of the interior and the commercial interests of the ports and seacoast), it passed a Judiciary bill (again after a fight over the powers of the executive, specifically of his right to dismiss an appointee after the appointee had been approved by the Senate), and it established the Departments of the Treasury, Foreign Affairs, and War.

Since Congress wouldn't reconvene until January, Adams wanted to go home to Braintree. Abigail, however, worn out by the constant visiting of Congressional members and their wives, and the dither of packing and unpacking and hiring servants, not to mention a natural desire to be near her new grandson, decided to stay in their New York home. John reluctantly gave in and visited Braintree alone. In December he returned with some Braintree butter and eggs, and with news of family and friends.

Once again they settled into their routine of political activities when the Senate reconvened for its second session in January. For John it meant presiding over the Senate each day, riding from their home in Richmond Hill, a mile north of the city, in a chaise each morning with his son Charles, who, at his father's urging, had been accepted for an internship in the law office of Alexander Hamilton. Adams' position as Vice-President also continued to entail many social obligations, including entertaining and being entertained, which he and Abigail found tiring.

In this second session of the Congress one of the major issues taken up was the issue of the funding of states' debts by the national government. Again, this was part of the larger issue of a strong central government versus states' rights, and it was the Federalists against the anti-Federalists, as the two factions came to be known. If the federal government took over the states' debts, it would make the federal government that much stronger. Leading the Federalists was the newly appointed Secretary of the Treasury Alexander Hamilton, while James Madison (one of the authors of *The Federalist Papers*, along with Hamilton and Jay) fought for his own version of a funding bill. The issue dragged on in the House for months, but in the end the Federalists won the day.

Another issue of considerable importance in the debates of the second session of Congress was where the capitol of the country was to be located. New York and Philadelphia, the largest cities, seemed the most natural sites for the new government, though Baltimore was also considered. Again, sectarian interests intervened. The Southern states were fearful of an increase in the power of the Northern states, whose interests differed from their own, if the capitol was located in the North. A compromise was finally reached in June, when Congress passed legislation naming Philadelphia as the new temporary capitol (for a period of ten years) while a new capitol was built on low ground near the Potomac (and not too far from Mt. Vernon, Washington's home).

One result of this decision to move the capitol was that the Adamses faced the daunting task once again of moving and setting up housekeeping in yet another house. The move was especially difficult for Abigail, for Nabby had given birth to a third child in August. It was another boy, and they named it Thomas. Abigail and John had also grown fond of their Richmond Hill home north of the city, with its thirty acres and view of the Hudson River. By the end of September, however, it was apparent the move could no longer be put off, and the arduous task of packing began.

The stress of all this activity, not to mention the thought of moving, undoubtedly contributed to making Abigail ill. By the end of October, when it was time move, she came down with a high fever that delayed their move for five days. Also, the rheumatism that had begun to plague her in her mid-forties made the journey, though they went by boat, unpleasant. Her one consolation was that their son Thomas Boylston, who had graduated from Harvard, would join them in Philadelphia to continue his study of the law.

In Philadelphia they rented a spacious house at Bush Hill, two miles outside the city. Abigail, however, worried about the expense of maintaining two homes and fixing up this new one, was not happy in Philadelphia. In addition, there was the worry of hiring and keeping good servants, many of whom, she was to find, drank too much. As a result, she lived there with John for only six months before returning home to Quincy.

She returned in the fall, but left again after a few months, vowing never to return to Philadelphia. And for the remaining five years of his vice-presidency, Adams lived alone in Philadelphia in rented rooms. He returned to Quincy after each session, usually early in March, and stayed until the end of November before returning to preside over the Senate when it reconvened.

One result of this was that Adams was pretty much left out of the loop as far as the administration was concerned. Washington rarely called upon him for advice, and when he considered doing so, invariably Adams was not there. Even Jefferson, as Secretary of State, only called on him twice for advice. All of which left Adams with the sense that his position was pretty much that of a nullity. He hated it, feeling "completely insignificant" and complaining of his "tedious days and lonesome nights" without Abigail. He even, in private letters, on occasion threatened to resign. But, of course, it was the usual bluster and bluff that was part of his nature. His strong sense of honor and duty would never have permitted him to do any such thing. In fact, at the end of his first term he actively sought reelection, aware that this was the best chance he had of succeeding Washington as President.

Returning to Philadelphia in November of 1790 and finding that Congress wouldn't reconvene for a month, Adams began writing a book called *Discourses on Davila*. It was based on the writings of an Italian historian, Henrico Caterino Davila, about the French civil wars of the sixteenth century. Quoting extensively from the Davila text, Adams' comments were meant to caution Americans (especially the anti-Federalists, now beginning to be known as Republicans) on the dangers in the excesses of the French Revolution (the Revolution had begun with the storming of the Bastille on July 14 of the previous year, but word only reached America in January of 1790).

What especially disturbed Adams about the French Revolution was the break-down in the balance of a tripartite government. He believed it essential in a republican form of government that there be a balance between a strong executive, a bicameral legislature, and an independent judiciary. It was what he had recommended for Massachusetts, and for the United States when it formed itself into a Union in 1787.

News of the Revolution, however, cheered the Republicans and the majority of Americans, who saw in it the spread of their own principles of liberty and freedom and a representative government. For John the Revolution signaled the breakdown of stable government and was an omen of bad things to come, which was not a popular view to take at the time, especially as Adams had his eye on the Presidency.

What was worse, Adams, to counter the idealism espoused by the French leaders of the Revolution in its backers among the Republicans and in the populace in his own country, took the occasion to reemphasize the fallibility of man and, in his realistic view, the fact of the general inequality of men (not before the law, of course, but in their God-given talents).

All men, he said, sought distinction, and unless a government and a society provided for this need by way of rituals and titles, it was fraught with danger to the stability of society. He asked the reader to consider the motivations for each man's actions, the ambitions and strivings for distinction that lay in each man's breast. While the hope for a republican form of government lay in an educated citizenry, knowledge and education would not be enough for the survival of that government if the passions of the human heart were not taken into account and channeled so they found an outlet in service to their fellow man and society.

He stressed that while men had the power to do good, they also had the power to do much evil. Again he emphasized that the best way to control the evil that men might do lay in the balance of the powers of government. It was what would make his own country function, grow, and prosper, and it was what was certainly *not* happening in the government being established in France.

There, any similarity between what had happened in America and what was happening in France ended, as far as Adams was concerned. He refused to indulge in the idealism that was stirring the breasts of his countrymen. In this he misjudged his readership. An outcry was raised against what was felt as an attack upon the French Revolution and its ideals, and the series of articles that made up the book were suspended from publication.

Adams, as was usual with him, was surprised and upset by the furor his articles, and subsequent book, aroused. He felt he was only speaking the plain truth, truth he claimed to find in Scripture. As far as he was concerned, he was only being forthright and honest, and the principles he espoused, and the cautions he noted, should be considered on those terms. Also, as was usual with him, his reactions had a tint of paranoia about them. In private letters, especially to his friend Benjamin Rush, he was cynical and self-pitying, and he complained of the lack of appreciation for his efforts and good intentions.

The third session of the new Congress convened in early December, with two new senators. Two days later Washington addressed the Congress. The next day the Senate received a packet of eulogiums from the French National Assembly on Benjamin Franklin, who had died a few months earlier.

Adams, as President of the Senate, was obliged to read these effusions to the assembly, which he did with ill grace, claiming to find the many honorary titles awarded Franklin in poor taste coming from a nation that had professed to do away with titles. The truth was he lacked the admiration for Franklin held by the public, both in France and in America, and was perhaps more than a little jealous, if not envious, of the attention being accorded him.

After that the Congress settled down to its business with, compared to the first two sessions, a remarkable lack of partisan bickering. Alexander Hamilton had submitted a plan for a national bank, which was easily passed, to the dismay of the anti-Federalists. Jefferson espoused a war upon the Barbary pirates, who would only cease their depredations (called *Algerian* because one of the principal North African nations involved was Algeria) upon American shipping upon the payment of bribes. And Washington had called for a strengthening of American troops to defend its frontiers. All of which increased the anxiety of the anti-Federalists at this strengthening of the Federal government.

In February the Congress passed an excise bill to raise taxes for the government. This, the anti-Federalists felt, was the most oppressive measure of all. It would enable the Federal government to reach into the pocket of every citizen, they reasoned, and soon there would be revenue officers scouring the country to collect revenue. This would be as bad, in their view, as what the British had tried to do. They blamed Hamilton, who somehow, they felt, had managed to get Congress to do his will. Worse, at the end of the long session, which lasted well into June, a dozen bills were passed without adequate debate or without even having been read.

Adams, however, was pleased. He felt the government had made more progress in two years than he could have possibly hoped. And in early July, when the weather permitted, he and Abigail headed back to Braintree, stopping off in New York for a brief visit with Nabby and their grandchildren.

Anxious to get home, they continued on their way after only a short visit. They looked forward to the quiet routines of Braintree, but, initially at least, were to be disappointed. They were celebrities in their home town now, and there were many visits from friends and relatives. They were not upset, however, because they figured they had the long summer ahead of them to settle down to the pleasures of rural life and the joy of being home.

Unfortunately, something happened to mar that pleasure: the publication of Thomas Paine's *Rights of Man*. It marked the beginning of a rift between Jefferson and Adams that was to last for a quarter of a century, until Dr. Benjamin Rush, one of the signers of the Declaration and a friend of both, urged a renewal of their friendship in 1812. They began then a correspondence that lasted until their deaths.

The *Rights of Man* was originally published in England in the spring of that year, but a Virginian by the name of John Beckley, clerk of the House, had gotten hold of a copy and had it published in the United States. Before doing so, he loaned the copy to James Madison, who passed it on to Jefferson. Jefferson, after reading it, sent the copy to the printer with a note saying that he was glad "something was at length to be publicly said against the political heresies which had of late sprung up among us."

Jefferson claimed, perhaps ingenuously, that he had not meant the note to be printed. But printed it was, as a preface to the edition. The "political heresies" to which he referred, as everyone knew when the book came out, were those contained in the *Discourses on Davila*. Adams, of course, touchy as always where his ego was concerned, was angered and hurt. Those who disliked Adams and what they called his "monarchal" principles were, on the other hand, quite delighted.

Jefferson claimed to be embarrassed by the furor his unauthorized introduction to Paine's book had caused, especially in the press (one anti-Federalist editor referred to Adams as "the Duke of Braintree"). But the fat was in the fire, and the worst was yet to come. While telling Washington he had not meant the note to be printed, Jefferson took the occasion to complain about Adams' "monarchical" leanings. And despite the furor, he did nothing to quiet it.

Adams, on the other hand, felt it would be inappropriate for him as Vice-President to respond either to the slurs contained in Secretary of State Jefferson's preface, or to the idealistic, and therefore dangerous, principles espoused in *The Rights of Man*. He didn't let it go at that, however. Since these principles undercut everything he had been saying in the *Davila*, he urged his son John Quincy to respond.

John Quincy wrote a series of articles that appeared in the Boston *Columbian Centinel* over the *nom de plume* of "Publicola." Widely assumed to have been written by Adams, they only increased the furor in the press. Jefferson, uncomfortable with the public uproar, wrote Adams a letter of apology – three months after the original indiscretion – saying it had never been his intention to have their names "brought before the public on this occasion." But never one to take a hard look at his own shortcomings, and lacking the courage for direct confrontation, he lay the blame for the controversy on the "Publicola" papers rather than his preface.

It wasn't much of an apology, but Adams was pleased by the friendly tone of Jefferson's letter and responded with a friendly letter of his own. Accepting Jefferson's explanation for the unintended publication of his note to the printer, he said that the printer had "sown the seeds of more evil than he can ever atone for."

Adams went on in his letter to deplore the dissemination of the false idea that he favored monarchy and aristocracy. He had never, he said, expressed or intimated such a thought "in any public or private letter." He challenged anyone to find a single instance of it in any of his works. He also assured Jefferson he had nothing to do with the writing or correction of the "Publicola" papers. The author of those papers, he wrote, "followed his own judgment, information, and discretion without any assistance from me."

Of course, neither man was being totally candid. Adams did not tell Jefferson that the papers had been written by his son, and Jefferson never admitted having told Washington prior to writing the letter to Adams that the "public heresies" he cited in his preface to the Paine pamphlet referred to the *Discourses*. In addition, before writing to Adams, Jefferson had been informed by Madison that the "Publicola" papers were *not* written by Adams.

The matter might have ended there, but Jefferson wrote again, insisting that the "Publicola" papers had been the cause of all their troubles. After that, any pretense of friendship between him and Adams was pretty much over. The truth was, the two-party system was beginning in earnest, and Adams and Jefferson were on either side of the political divide that was forming.

On one side were Hamilton and, because he was an advocate of a strong federal government, Adams, and on the other were Jefferson and Madison. These two factions, or "parties," were the Federalists and the Republicans (the name the anti-Federalists finally chose to avoid the negative "anti"). The Republicans wanted less government, with a shift of power downward to the people through their representatives in Congress; they were inclined to favor the South and rural interests. The Federalists wanted a strong executive and a strengthening of the federal government; they were inclined to favor the Northern states and mercantile interests.

The rift widened a year later when Jefferson and Madison started a newspaper, edited by the Southern poet Philip Freneau, called the *National Gazette*. Its purpose, at least initially, was to promulgate republican views; but it wasn't long before the paper, not content with lofty, philosophical disquisitions, began launching personal attacks against the administration, especially against Hamilton. Even Washington came in for some personal attacks. Adams, however, keeping a low profile in the Senate (he rarely participated in the debates now), managed to escape most of them.

When Adams returned to Philadelphia in September of 1791, the factionalism was papered over with good manners and affability among the members of the Congress. Adams, though sick with a return of the disease he had had in The Netherlands, again took his seat in the Senate and presided over their deliberations, keeping order by tapping on the desk with his silver pen.

Trouble on the frontier with the Indians induced general agreement that the army should be increased to five thousand, along with an increase in the required expenditures; and a tariff to raise the money was passed. It was also generally agreed that the number of representatives in the House should be increased. But here factionalism again kicked in, not so much between the Federalists and Republicans, but between the North and the South.

Negro slaves were not considered citizens when it came to voting rights, yet the Southern states wanted them counted as part of their populations when it came to representation in the House. Obviously, this was not something the Northern states found acceptable. In forming the Union, the rift between the pro-slavery and anti-slavery (abolitionist) factions had been papered over. Now there seemed no way of avoiding the issue.

Members of Congress on both sides of the divide, aware of the fragility of the Union and the need to preserve it, worked out a compromise: A slave, they decided, would count as 3/5^{ths} of a citizen in a census of the population for determining representation. It was a compromise that worked for the time being, though the issue of slavery would remain a canker in the body politic and nation that wouldn't be resolved until the Civil War, seventy years later.

The basic conflict between the Federalists and Republicans over governance worsened in the months leading up to the second presidential election of November 1792, with much scheming and mud-slinging. Adams, home in Braintree (now renamed Quincy), delayed his return to Philadelphia lest he appear eager for reelection, despite talk that Governor George Clinton of New York was actively seeking the post of Vice-President. Washington, who was above party, had agreed to run for a second term, but Clinton was a Republican, and Hamilton would have none of that.

He pleaded with Adams to return before the elections, when the Senate reconvened. Adams, though ambitious for the post and aware the vice-presidency would lead to the presidency, had an earnest desire to remain above the fray. He hated party politics and the intrigue it entailed, and was determined to stay out of it by remaining in Braintree until after the elections. He also had personal reasons for doing so. Abigail was going through her change of life and was not feeling well, and he himself had developed a touch of palsy (his hands now shook). In addition, he had a genuine love of the peace and quiet of Braintree and the home he now called "Peacefield."

Despite the machinations of the Republicans and the politicking of Clinton and those around him, Adams still came in second after Washington in electoral votes, retaining his position as Vice-President (Clinton got 50 electoral votes, not enough to unseat Adams). The Republicans, however, strengthened their position in the general election, most notably by gaining seats in the House. There was no question now that Jefferson was their leader, that his political strength was on the rise, and that he would be a force to reckon with in future elections.

The politicking got worse in Washington's second term, as did the attacks on the President himself. Those close to him would see his face grow white with anger as he read some of these personal attacks in the newspapers, though he kept his cool in public. Jefferson, a behind-the-scenes instigator of many of the attacks against the administration, resigned his post as Secretary of State in December of 1793. But while supposedly in retirement at Monticello, he kept in touch via letters with Madison and others who were doing the maneuvering to further the Republican cause.

One of the issues in this second term about which political controversy swirled was the appointment in 1793 by the newly declared republic of France of a young man named Edmond Charles Genêt as minister to the United States. France had recently declared war against Britain and Holland, and Genêt's job was to gain the support of the United States, its ally by the treaty of 1778.

As if this wasn't enough to stir up trouble, Genêt, landing in Charleston, South Carolina, in April of 1794 and ignoring protocol, commissioned privateers to prey on British shipping, and made plans to raise an army under the command of George Rogers Clark to help the French. He met with huge popular support in his journey north to Philadelphia, especially by the Republicans.

His mistake lay in assuming this was the will of the administration. To forestall him, Washington, after consulting with Hamilton and Jefferson, issued a proclamation of Neutrality on April 22, before Genêt arrived in Philadelphia. It reflected Washington's firm belief that his country should engage in "no foreign entanglements," a stand Adams also favored, and had for many years.

The administration's "out" as far as the treaty with France was concerned lay in the fact that the treaty specified mutual aid in the event of an attack or declaration of war against either country. In this case it was France that had declared the war. Also, since France had undergone a revolution, it was not the same country with which the United States had signed the treaty. Therefore, as Adams wrote to Tench Coxe, Hamilton's assistant in the Treasury Department who had kept him informed of proceedings, the United States was free "from all moral obligation to fulfill the treaty."

After four weeks, when Genêt finally reached Philadelphia, he was widely acclaimed by a huge throng, and in particular by Jefferson, who assured him that the American peoples' sympathies lay with France. Jefferson also assured him that the vast majority of them would accept and support him. Unfortunately, that majority did not include President Washington. He received Genêt, but coolly and formally. By August, because of Genêt's shenanigans, the Cabinet had demanded his recall, and those who had accepted him so warmly were quick to disassociate themselves from him, including Jefferson.

The "Citizen Genêt" affair, as it came to be called, had hardly ended, however, when another furor was stirred up. This time it was by the British. Not content with blockading France and seizing some of the smaller French islands, they proclaimed their right to seize any vessels, even those of neutral countries, doing business with the French in the West Indies. By the following spring almost 250 American vessels had been seized, stirring up cries for war, especially in the Congress.

Washington, anxious to avoid war, announced he was sending John Jay to England as a special envoy to open British ports to American trade and to resolve their differences vis-à-vis France. The war fever gradually abated as the country waited word of the success or failure of Jay's mission. Unfortunately, the treaty Jay finally sent to Philadelphia a year later only stirred things up again. It secured few concessions from the British, while granting many.

The principle British concession was removal of their troops from their outposts on the Western frontier. In return, they expected the United States not to impose duties on the British, to settle the prewar claims of British creditors, and to permit the British and its Indian allies to continue to trap and trade in the Northwest. Worse, the treaty said nothing about the slaves taken from America by the British, nor anything about the impressment of American sailors seized from American ships for service in the British navy.

Copies of the treaty were given to the Senate for their consideration, for they would have to approve it before it could go into effect. The Senators were enjoined by the President not to disclose the terms of the treaty to the outside world while it was being discussed. But someone leaked a copy to the Philadelphia *Aurora,* a leading Republican newspaper, and all hell broke loose. Rioting mobs in New York and Philadelphia hung Jay in effigy as a traitor, and Washington was castigated in the newspapers. Jefferson joined the fray with a friendly letter to the French ambassador.

Washington called the Senate to a special session in June of 1795 to discuss the treaty. Adams, who returned to Philadelphia from Braintree to preside over the session, called it one of the most rancorous he had ever attended. The angry debates went on for thirteen days before the Federalists were finally able to muster the two-thirds majority required for ratification of the treaty.

Adams, as president of the Senate, did not, and was not called upon to, enter the debate. His feeling, as it was of the majority that finally passed the bill, was that a flawed treaty was better than none at all, since the alternative might well be all out war with Britain, a confrontation that was daunting to most of the Senators.

The treaty soothed the British but sent U.S.-French relations spiraling to a new low. The French Directory, in July of 1796, asserted their right to seize neutral shipping, as had Britain, and began depredations upon American ships. Feelings ran high, not just among the public but in the Congress. It was a tumultuous time that lasted well into the next year, and into the months leading up to the election, when the House finally passed the appropriations needed to put the treaty into effect.

Meanwhile, most members of Washington's cabinet had resigned or been replaced, including Hamilton. Even Edmund Randolph, who had replaced Jefferson as Secretary of State, was forced to resign, accused of taking bribes from the French. Chances are Washington would not have served a third term as President in any event, but the furor in the press, the bickering within the administration, and the back-stabbing that went on during his second term may have hastened his decision.

Washington made every attempt to remain above the fray, never giving any indication he would not serve again. Adams, however, had been officially informed that he would not run when he returned for the Congressional session in December of 1795. The world at large only learned of Washington's decision not to run again when he published his Farewell Address (written largely by Madison, with help from Hamilton) in a Philadelphia newspaper, September 19, 1796.

As soon as the decision was announced, the speculations began, both in public and in private, as to who would be chosen to succeed him. Adams was the obvious choice, though he went through the usual dither of whether to serve his country (he thought it his "duty") or retire and live a peaceful life in "a very humble Style." He pretended indifference as to whether he was considered for the presidency or not, saying it made no difference to him. When the time came, however, it was clear Adams fully expected the Federalists to support him.

What he didn't know, and was never consulted about, was that Thomas Pinckney from South Carolina had been selected for second place to "balance the slate" (as Jefferson sagely observed), because he was from the South. Adams, if he had known, would have been distressed. While Pinckney had a distinguished war record in the Revolution (he had even been wounded and captured at Camden), and had served as Ambassador to England and very successfully as envoy to Spain, he hardly had the qualifications Adams deemed essential for high office.

In fact, Adams considered him a "nobody." For the moment, however, he had another worry. It was clear the Republicans wanted Jefferson to succeed Washington (Aaron Burr was their choice for vice-president), and Adams was concerned that he himself might come in second and, under the rules then prevailing, become Vice-President again. While ambitious to be President, he was determined not to serve under Jefferson, for whom, by this time, he had lost much of his respect.

Writing to Abigail on January 6, 1794, when Jefferson was leaving for Monticello after having resigned as Secretary of State in December, Adams said that Jefferson's "want of candor, his obstinate prejudices both of aversion and attachments; his real partiality in spite of all his pretensions, and his low notions about many things, have so utterly reconciled me to it that I will not weep" at his going.

Not that Jefferson was silent or inactive in "retirement." He kept in constant touch with Madison and others through letters, and did all he could behind the scenes to strengthen his own chances for the presidency and weaken the chances of Federalist candidates. So effective was he that Adams was concerned the coming election might be so close it would be decided in the House, where the Republicans had gained strength, and Jefferson would win.

The election *was* close, but not as close as Adams had predicted. After the electoral votes had been tabulated, they were sent to the Senate in a sealed envelope. It was Adams himself, as President of the Senate, who, on February 6, 1797, opened the envelope and read the results to the assembly. He had beaten Jefferson by three electoral votes, 71 to 68 (Pinckney had come in third). This meant John Adams was to be President of the United States of America, succeeding Washington, and Jefferson Vice-President.

Chapter Nine
President Adams (1797-1798)

With some trepidation, Adams waited through the winter months for his inauguration, which was to take place on March 4, 1797. Two things occurred, however that pleasantly surprised him. The first was the cessation of the vituperation and attacks against him in the press. Even more surprising was the change in tone to praise and acceptance and well-wishing; it was as if no one, except the most partisan, had ever been against his candidacy. The second was word received through intermediaries that Jefferson had gracefully accepted defeat and would be happy to serve under him.

For the moment at least, it looked like the rabid partisanship he had dreaded would not occur, and that the country, and his administration, would be able to move forward on a steady course. What he didn't know was that the worst of any divisiveness that might occur during his term of office would come through Hamilton, who was already working behind the scenes to exercise control over his administration and the policies it might pursue.

Probably the worst mistake Adams made when he took office (which he later admitted) was keeping on as members of his Cabinet those who had served under Washington. His thinking was that the transition to a new administration under his leadership would go more smoothly if the old members were retained. But most of those members, it turned out, were under the influence, if not the control, of Hamilton, who had ambitions of his own.

Unknown to Adams, Hamilton had maneuvered behind the scenes to increase the vote count for Pinckney, under whom he would have preferred to serve, even at the risk of a split that would have meant the defeat of the Federalists and the election of Jefferson as President. In addition, the trouble with France, which had begun long before Adams took office, would bring this divisiveness in his cabinet, fomented by Hamilton, to a head.

Relations with France had been deteriorating since the Genêt fracas, and the Jay treaty had convinced the French that the United States had come under the influence of Great Britain, despite the continuing British raids on U.S. shipping. As a result, the Directory issued a decree on July 4, 1796, which stated that they would treat neutral vessels in the Caribbean the same as did the British; and the French began their own depredations on neutral ships and property in that area.

A month before Adams took office, a list of American vessels and property plundered, compiled by Secretary of State Pickering at Washington's behest, indicated that the cost of French depredations had mounted to catastrophic proportions. Even before being sworn in Adams was being entreated to send a special envoy to France to deal with the matter. Two days before his inauguration he consulted with Jefferson on the possibility of Jefferson accepting the mission. Jefferson declined on the basis that it would be inappropriate for the

Vice President to be out of the country for the length of time it might take to resolve the matter; Adams agreed.

Shortly after his' inauguration, things had gotten so bad it was not clear if *any* peace envoy was advisable. Word reached Philadelphia that the French, incensed by the Jay treaty, felt it abrogated all ties between their two nations. Charles Pinckney, the U.S. Ambassador to France, had been declared *persona non grata* and forced to leave the country (he took refuge in The Netherlands). There was even talk of war, all of which greatly exacerbated the divisiveness within the Congress, the administration, and between the political parties then forming.

The Federalists, and Hamilton in particular, were anti-French and wanted closer ties with Great Britain; the Republicans, and Jefferson in particular, were anti-British and wanted closer ties with France. Each side accused Adams, whose aim was to avoid war and at the same time preserve national honor and dignity, of dereliction of duty. It was a no-win situation, with the Republicans accusing Adams of fomenting war, and the Federalists accusing Adams of toadying to the French.

To deal with this first great crisis of his administration Adams, following the example of Washington, called a cabinet meeting to solicit the advice of his department heads, unaware that each of his cabinet officials, except Attorney General Charles Lee, had contacted Hamilton for instructions on how to proceed in the situation. Adams was therefore pleasantly surprised at their unanimity in backing his efforts to do all he could to avoid war.

The cabinet members even agreed with Adams' decision to send a special commission to Paris to work out a resolution or treaty. But again, unknown to him, they were influenced by Hamilton's thinking, which was that if it came to war the dispatch of a special commission would at least demonstrate that the Federalists had done all they could to avoid it.

With his cabinet agreed on a course of action, Adams issued a summons for Congress to reconvene on May 15 to consider the matter. Addressing them at noon on the second day, he began by belaboring the French for their war-like actions, in particular their treatment of Pinckney and their depredations on U.S. vessels and property in the Caribbean. He emphasized the United States' desire for peace, but warned that the U.S. was prepared to go to war if necessary; and he urged Congress to vote monies to expand the navy, enlist a militia, and strengthen their port fortifications.

Finally, the main reason for calling Congress into special session, Adams asked them to approve sending a commission of three men to France to try to resolve the issue and obtain a commercial treaty similar to the one John Jay had negotiated with the British. The men he named were Charles Pinckney, who was still in Europe, John Marshall (a federal judge he later appointed Chief Justice of the Supreme Court), and Elbridge Gerry, an old friend in whom he had complete trust, who happened to be a Republican.

The speech, in general, pleased the Federalists (though there was an uproar over the appointment of Gerry); but it outraged the Republicans, who felt its bellicose tones presaged war. Hamilton, always more politically astute than most, was especially pleased that the Republican Elbridge Gerry had been appointed to the commission. To his way of thinking, it meant the Republicans would be forced to share the blame if the peace efforts failed.

Congress debated these issues for almost two months before finally agreeing to most of what Adams had proposed, including the three members of the special commission. It agreed to strengthen the navy by adding twelve new frigates, but defeated a proposal to strengthen the army by fifteen thousand men.

After Congress dissolved, the two commissioners residing in the States, Marshall and Gerry, left in July, each by a different port, to join Pinckney in Paris, where they planned to meet with the wily, newly-appointed Talleyrand, recently returned to France after two years exile in America to become French Foreign Minister

When Congress ended its session, Abigail and John returned to "Peacefield," as they now called their home in Quincy, where they hoped to spend a fairly peaceful summer. In this they were not disappointed. There was no word from France, either good or bad, as to the fate of the commission, and the political climate, for the moment, had lost its bite.

The sensational news of the summer, which made the headlines, involved a scandal Hamilton had gotten himself into with a married woman. The news, though it pleased the Republicans and upset the Federalists, didn't particularly disturb the President or Abigail. The good news of the summer, for them, which they received shortly before leaving for Philadelphia in early October, came in a letter from John Quincy.

In the letter John Quincy announced his marriage on July 26 to a young American woman named Louisa Johnson, who resided in London with her parents. John and Abigail were, of course, delighted. Abigail's only concern was that, because Louisa's parents were wealthy and she had lived in Europe most of her life, she might be spoiled by her upbringing and therefore unable to adapt to the plainness of their own style of living.

As the Adamses neared New York that autumn on their way to Philadelphia, word reached them that the annual outbreak of fever and its attendant illness had not yet abated, and that the opening of the new session of Congress had been delayed because few of the congressmen had returned to the city.

They decided to stay with Nabby and their grandchildren in East Chester until Congress was ready to meet again. But it was not a happy visit. Colonel Smith was away, presumably on business, though Nabby knew not where, leaving her and the children in distressed circumstances. Her parents wanted them to come with them to Philadelphia, but, dutiful wife that she was, she refused.

Congress finally convened two weeks late, in the third week of November. Adams' state of the union address, which he gave on the 23rd, was pessimistic. There was no news from France on the fate of the mission, but alarming news about Napoleon's victories (there was even talk of him invading Britain) made Adams prepare the country for the worst. While he did not expect war with France, he was not sanguine about the reception of the commissioners, nor, if they *were* received, on the outcome of their negotiations; and he again urged Congress to vote the monies needed to strengthen the country's defense capabilities.

Next, he sought the advice of his Cabinet on the best way to proceed in the crisis should the commission fail in its endeavors, or if something worse should befall them. There was general agreement that war should be avoided if at all possible, and that at least one of the envoys, should they fail in their mission, be kept in Europe to demonstrate America's continued willingness to discuss its differences with France. It was also agreed that the United States should proceed with the proposed military preparations.

On March 4, 1798, a year after taking office, Adams finally received word from Pinckney, Marshall, and Gerry, via coded dispatches sent to Secretary of State Pickering, that Talleyrand had refused to receive them. Worse, they had been approached by secret agents (the envoys did not name them, identifying them only as W, X, Y, and Z), who demanded a personal bribe (a *douceur,* they called it, a "sweetener"). They wanted $250,000 for Talleyrand if negotiations were to be opened, and also demanded that Adams apologize for what they perceived as anti-French comments in his address to Congress. In addition to that, they wanted the United States to extend France a loan of $10,000,000.

Adams, of course, was outraged, as was Pickering. But in passing the news along to Congress, he merely noted the failure of the mission and urged Congress to reconsider the recommendations he had made to them for strengthening United States defenses. Of the indignities to which the envoys had been subjected he did not at that time inform them. Among his cabinet members, however, who were privy to the dispatches, there was already great division as to the steps Adams should take. Some even urged war.

The Republicans in Congress, not taking the news well, and wary of possible duplicity, accused Adams of fomenting war and of withholding information that would portray the situation in a more favorable light. They insisted the full dispatches be released. Adams, fearing the lives of the envoys might be put in jeopardy if the full extent of the scurrility of Talleyrand and his agents was revealed, at first refused. But when a number of Federalists, aware of their contents, joined in demanding a full disclosure, Adams reluctantly gave in, assuming the envoys were now out of danger.

It was a grave error on the part of the Republicans, for the contents of the dispatches revealed the situation to be much worse than anyone had imagined. At first Congress tried to keep the information within the House and Senate, but when the news leaked out, it was agreed to publish and distribute 50,000 copies of the dispatches. The result was public outrage against the French.

It began in Philadelphia, and spread like wildfire throughout the States. With it the slogan "Millions for defense but not one cent for tribute," which had appeared in a Philadelphia newspaper, also spread from person to person. As a result all favorable sentiment for the French disappeared. No one dared display any longer the French tricolor cockade on their hat, as had been the Republican fashion, nor sing patriotic French songs as had the "Jacobins," the people in this country who supported the French Revolution.

Adams himself was never more popular. He was feted by many individuals and groups, who praised him for the steadiness of his resolve and pledged their support for any actions he might take, even if they led to war. But the major result of the "XYZ Affair," as it came to be known, was that Congress, after much debate, finally passed the legislation strengthening U.S. defenses Adams requested.

Merchant vessels were armed and empowered to capture any French privateers found in American waters, a "provisional" army of 10,000 men was authorized, and bills were passed strengthening port fortifications. Even more to Adams' liking, Congress passed a bill establishing a Department of the Navy that was separate from the Department of War. It was Adams' pleasure to appoint Benjamin Stoddert of Maryland, a friend and ally whose trust and loyalty he felt he could count on, as the Secretary of the Navy.

The next problem Adams faced that spring and summer was the appointment of someone to command the army that Congress had established, and the appointment of general officers to serve under him. The first appointment was pretty much a no-brainer. George Washington was assumed to be the only choice; in fact, Adams would have faced a hailstorm of criticism if it had not been his first choice. The question was, would Washington, who had retired from political life to manage his estates at Mount Vernon, would be willing to serve?

To find out, Adams sent James McHenry, his Secretary of War, to Mount Vernon in early July, along with a list of general officers who might serve under him. Washington, though he had reservations, agreed to become commander-in-chief of the new army, with the proviso he not serve actively in the field unless there was the threat of imminent invasion. He also agreed to choose the general officers from the list Adams had submitted, but insisted that he alone would decide the order of their rank.

The latter condition was a breach of the President's powers, but Adams temporized, merely citing the Constitution in his reply. Part of him, aware it would be a difficult and delicate task that would subject him to considerable pressure and criticism, would gladly have let Washington decide the ranking of the general officers. But he feared Washington would choose Hamilton as second-in-command, which he felt would be a catastrophe for the country.

By now he was fully aware of Hamilton's influence on his Cabinet and his many machinations behind the scenes to subvert his policies. He considered him overly ambitious, even *power-hungry,* and not to be trusted. Adams had always been fearful of a standing army, and God forbid it should come under the control of Hamilton. Washington, it was generally conceded, was too old for active service and would leave the decision-making in the field to his second in command, who most likely would be Hamilton.

Meanwhile, amidst the war hysteria, Congress passed legislation that Adams had not requested, but which he nevertheless signed into law. These were the so-called Alien and Sedition Acts. They were a grievous mistake, for they not only caused an uproar (not just among the Republicans), but cast a shadow on Adams' term of office that has persisted to this day.

The four acts included a Naturalization Act extending the years of residency needed to obtain American citizenship from 5 to 14 years; two Alien Acts giving the President the power to deport "dangerous" foreigners; and, most damaging of all, a Sedition Act giving the President the power to jail or fine anyone who wrote anything "false, scandalous, or malicious against the government," or who did anything to "stir up sedition."

The furor these Acts aroused in the nation at large was hard for Adams to live down. Kentucky and Virginia passed resolutions, authored by Jefferson it was subsequently learned, which stated that any State had the right to nullify any act of Congress they considered unconstitutional. The resolutions were widely circulated, and heightened the on-going battle between those favoring States' rights and those favoring a strong central government. Adams himself came in for much vilification.

In an attempt to allay the country's fears, Adams stressed the fact that the Acts were due to expire at the end of his term. They were, he said, merely temporary "war acts" necessary for defending the country at this time of crisis (i.e., the quasi-war with the French). In the end, he never used the Alien Acts, although he did use the Sedition Act to shut down five Republican newspapers he considered the most scurrilous in their attacks on him and his administration. The Republicans cried "tyranny," as did much of the public, and the Acts remained an issue that contributed to Adams' loss of a second term when he ran against Jefferson.

The Congress, because of these exertions, was late in adjourning; and the heat and dust of summer had already set in when John and Abigail began their slow, arduous journey by carriage back to

Quincy. They stopped off briefly in East Chester to see Nabby and the grandchildren, and by the time they arrived home they were mentally and physically exhausted. Abigail had come down with a mysterious illness with flu-like symptoms (now believed to have been malaria) that necessitated her being put to bed when they finally reached home.

Despite the ministrations of doctors from Boston, she did not get well and was confined to her room for eleven weeks, so sick at times that John despaired for her life. It was, he wrote, one of the "gloomiest" summers he had ever spent. He was so worried that little federal business got done. Only toward the end of September was he able to see visitors and attend to the business of state by writing letters and signing documents.

It wasn't until November 6 that Abigail was well enough to come downstairs for the first time. A little more than a week later John began his journey back to Philadelphia for the opening of the new session of Congress, this time, as he wrote to Abigail, alone and miserable. The good news, for him, was that the crisis with France had begun to subside.

He had had intimations of this when Gerry, landing in Boston from Europe in September, reported to him at Quincy that the French Directorate was sounding less truculent and more willing to make peace. When he arrived in Philadelphia, he heard the same from a private citizen, a Quaker named George Logan, who had spent two weeks in Paris on his own seeking peace. Logan was castigated in the press for interfering in affairs of state, and spurned by members of Congress and the Cabinet, but Adams served him tea and listened to what he had to say.

Soon after that Adams received news from abroad, via dispatches from both William Vans Murray, his ambassador at The Hague, and his son John Quincy, that the mood of the French had indeed undergone a change. The real convincer, however, was the news, which had been rumored for months but was not officially received in the capitol until New Year's, that Admiral Horatio Nelson had bottled up and destroyed the French fleet in the Mediterranean waters off the coast of Egypt, removing any capacity France might have for war against the United States.

Despite that, the pressure in Congress and among Federalists for Adams to declare war remained high, and because of the tough stance he had taken in previous addresses, it was going to be difficult for him to back down. Unless France made direct overtures, which was unlikely, he had to find a means of seeking the peace he had all along so ardently desired.

There seemed to be three avenues open to him: he could negotiate discretely with the French on a lower diplomatic level through Murray at The Hague, which would provide a face-saving device if anything went wrong, since no principals were involved. Secondly, he could insist the French send an envoy to Philadelphia, which was the toughest stance; or, third, he could send an envoy to Paris, which could be the riskiest if the envoy should be snubbed.

Adams chose the third way, his actions bolstered by a letter from Washington saying the country could not afford war and advising him to seek peace. To prepare the Congress, and the country, for peace overtures, Adams addressed Congress on December 7. Everyone was expecting him to request a declaration of war. Instead, after reiterating the U.S. desire for peace and the need to maintain strong defenses, he announced he would send a peace mission to Paris if the French assured him the U.S. envoys would be received with the protocol due a sovereign nation.

It was a speech that angered almost everyone – the Federalists who had been expecting a declaration of war, and the Republicans who found the tone of Adams' speech still too bellicose. Angered most were the two arch enemies, the Federalist Alexander Hamilton and the Republican Thomas Jefferson. Each of them had plans and personal ambitions that would be frustrated if Adams succeeded in his peace endeavors.

Hamilton had his eye on the army, which would be his to lead in the event of war, and possibly to use to achieve other objectives he had in mind, such as taking Florida, and possibly Louisiana, from the Spanish. There were even rumors he wanted to invade South America. Jefferson, for his part, had his eye on the Presidency, which he fully expected the Republicans to win if the present stalemate with France continued.

Adams' speech took the wind out of both their sails. The High Federalists, as they were called, could express their anger, but the Republicans, and Jefferson in particular, since Adams only did what they had been asking, had to muffle their response, giving him as little credit as possible for his peace-seeking initiative.

Chapter Ten
President Adams (1799-1801)

For the next two months, nothing happened; there was still no word from France. Then, on February 18, 1799, Adams, without consulting anyone, not even Abigail, took a bold and decisive step. He nominated William Vans Murray, their minister at The Hague, to be "minister plenipotentiary of the United States to the French Republic," notifying Congress, then in session, of the appointment by means of a courier.

Adams said he awaited their "advise and consent." At the same time he assured them he would not instruct Murray to proceed to Paris until he had received "direct and unequivocal assurances" from the French government, specifically the Minister of Foreign Relations, that Murray would be received with the respect and protocol due an envoy from a sovereign nation.

The message astounded Jefferson, who interrupted the Senate proceedings he was chairing to read it to the assembled Senators. Even the Federalists were taken aback, and momentarily stunned into silence. Jefferson's first response, privately, was to call it the "event of events." In public, however, he played down its importance, and only grudgingly gave Adams credit for his initiative, something Jefferson had long been urging him to do..

The attacks by the Federalists on the other hand, including many in his own Cabinet, were vicious. Some even wished him dead. But none dared vote against the appointment, for it would have been political suicide. Despite all their fuming, the best the Federalists could do, following the advice of Hamilton, was to urge Adams to send more than one envoy on the mission.

They claimed Murray was "not strong enough for so immensely important a mission." In actuality, they were hoping to subvert the mission by possibly causing divisiveness among its members. Adams, to ensure the confirmation of Murray, which was in doubt, finally gave in and nominated two additional envoys: Patrick Henry of Virginia and Oliver Ellsworth, the Chief Justice appointed by Washington who had sworn Adams into office. When Henry declined to serve because of age, Adams chose William Davie, the Federalist governor of North Carolina.

After confirming the envoys, Congress adjourned, and at the end of March 1799 Adams was at last able to return to Peacefield to look after his still ailing wife. Though Abigail felt better, she was still weak, had trouble sleeping, and was not up to any exertion. Adams, in addition to seeing to her comfort and needs, was glad to be home to superintend the work on his farm.

He could not, however, escape the many duties thrust upon him. While he enjoyed a few public appearances in Boston, where he was feted, he was irritated by the many visitors who called upon him at Quincy unannounced, and he was rude to many, even to some who came on affairs of state.

His stay in Quincy that year was so long that there was much grumbling, not just from the Federalists, but from the Congress and his Cabinet, about the length of time he spent away from the nation's Capitol. His response was that, with the modern system of couriers carrying the post back and forth, he had no trouble keeping up with the affairs of state from Quincy.

He pointed to Washington's many absences from the capitol. But the truth was, Washington was seldom away from the Capitol for more than two months; and in eight years in office, the longest he was ever away was three months. But for Adams it was routine to be back in Quincy when Congress was not in session, which for most of his term was much of the year.

There was a handicap, however, in being isolated from the Capitol. With no one around on whom to rely, he had to make most decisions on his own. One of these was to send the peace commissioners to France that Congress had authorized. The main reason for doing this was that, included in a dispatch from Murray at The Hague, there was a letter from Talleyrand assuring Adams that any envoys he sent to Paris would be cordially received.

Without consulting anyone, Adams announced that Davie and Ellsworth, the two peace envoys residing in the United States, would soon sail for Europe to join Murray. He directed Secretary of State Pickering to prepare instructions for them. But Pickering, who could have completed the assignment in a day or two, was not in favor of the mission, and he delayed a full month before writing to Adams to say he thought the mission should be postponed.

His excuse was that an uprising in France that summer had changed the composition of the Directorate and made sending the mission inadvisable. He inferred the whole Cabinet was in favor of the delay. In actuality, only two members agreed with him. This was something he could not have gotten away with if Adams had been on the scene. Not being there to consult with his other Cabinet members, and unaware of the political infighting going on, Adams agreed to postpone the departure of the mission.

Even so, Adams was reluctant to return to the Capitol before November, when Congress was to begin its new session. Only urgent appeals from Secretary of the Navy Stoddert at the end of August, and again at the beginning of September, warning Adams that "designing" men in his administration were attempting to take over foreign policy and subvert his peace mission, made him decide to return early.

Adams wrote to Pickering that he would arrive in Trenton, a small town in New Jersey that was being used as the temporary Capitol since Philadelphia was still being ravaged by the epidemic, by October 15. In his letter he made it clear he expected to meet with his assembled Cabinet at that time to discuss the matter of the mission to France.

He left Quincy for the Capitol on the last day of September, stopping in East Chester on the way for a brief visit with Nabby. There he learned the sad news that his alcoholic son Charles had disappeared, leaving his penniless wife Sally and their two small daughters on Nabby's hands, as if Nabby didn't have enough problems of her own, with a shiftless husband who was seldom home.

Highly distressed, and ill now with a cold, Adams pressed on to Trenton to take care of affairs of state, in particular to see that his peace mission directive was carried out. He arrived a few days early, expecting to meet only with his Cabinet. Instead, he found Hamilton, now a Major General in command of the troops at Newark, waiting for him.

This was strictly against protocol; a general officer had no business offering his commander-in-chief unsolicited advice. And Adams could have sent him packing. Instead, he listened patiently to Hamilton's at times overwrought diatribe against the French, and his urgent pleas for the British, for several hours before politely dismissing him, concluding that Hamilton was out of touch with reality. His partisan plea only confirmed Adams' decision to send the commissioners to Paris as soon as possible.

Even after several meetings with his Cabinet, including an especially lengthy one on the 15th that lasted long into the evening, at which only Stoddert (Lee had written a strong letter recommending the mission) took his side, Adams could not be dissuaded. The next day, October 16, he ordered Ellsworth and Davie, the two members of the peace mission still in the States, to sail within two weeks. He did this knowing it would cost him a second term.

Keeping the country out of war with France at this time of crisis was perhaps the greatest achievement of Adams' term in office. It is ironic that this great achievement was the chief cause of his failure to be reelected. But the sad truth, then as now, is that war and the patriotic fervor it arouses tends to guarantee the reelection of the incumbent. It was John Adams' great wisdom to know this, and a reflection of his great character that, knowing this, he pursued peace anyhow for the greater good of the nation.

The major reason this action was so detrimental to Adams was that it alienated his base among the Federalists. Despite his wish to distance himself from partisan politics, he knew their backing was essential for reelection. To be fair, there were other factors: the Alien and Sedition Acts, the inroads of Republicanism in New York (where the ambitious Aaron Burr did much to stir the seeds of discontent), and the imposition of direct taxes to support the strengthened military so essential for avoiding war also played a key role in Adams' failure to be reelected.

The seat of government moved from its temporary quarters in Trenton back to Philadelphia at the start of November. By then the epidemic had ceased taking its toll and members of the Congress had started drifting back to the Capitol. Adams met Abigail by arrangement in Brunswick, New Jersey. She had stopped in East Chester for a brief visit with Nabby on her way from Quincy.

After meeting her husband in Brunswick, she and John packed up their belongings in Trenton and moved to the Presidential mansion in Philadelphia that same month. Back in the capitol, Abigail, recovered from her illness, was caught up once again in a swirl of social duties as First Lady. This time, however, she found that, having become more proficient in such duties, she on occasion actually enjoyed them.

For Adams the press of duties had lessened somewhat. Partly as a result of this, the tone of his third annual address to Congress, on December 3, was moderate and pacific. It would be some time before the members of the peace mission were heard from, but he was hopeful; and his address to the Congress reflected this more sanguine mood, though he still urged them to pass the strong defense measures the nation would need if war occurred. .

During this lull, when the Congress was quiet and no new legislation was being considered, except for an attempt by the Republicans to have the Alien Acts rescinded, the news arrived in Philadelphia that George Washington had died on December 14 and been buried at his home at Mount Vernon on the 16th. His age at the time was 67. His death had been caused by a streptococcal infection of the throat following a cold. The nation was stunned.

The news arrived in the Capitol on the evening of December 17, and the next day the Congress shut down and the Capitol was draped in black. There was an outpouring of eulogies from every State in the Union. On the official day of mourning, the day after Christmas, there was a funeral procession in which thousands participated. Afterwards, hundreds of people, including John and Abigail, gathered in the small Anglican Church to participate in a solemn service, and in the evening John and Abigail hosted a dinner at the Presidential mansion for selected dignitaries.

Despite the outpouring of national grief and apparent unity, the political wars began again in earnest after the New Year holiday. 1800 was an election year, and the Republican attacks on the administration increased. Unfortunately, so did the bickering and political in-fighting among the Federalists in Adams' Cabinet.

Also, word reached the United States in February that General Bonaparte had seized the reins of power in France the previous November and declared himself "first consul." And despite the fact that the Republicans had been so pro-French, the public was not fazed. It was clear the Republicans were in the ascendancy and that Jefferson would be elected President.

To further their political cause, the Republicans seized on another issue in March, and made a to-do over what came to be called "the Thomas Nash affair." Thomas Nash, an English sailor accused of murder and mutiny, had taken refuge in Charleston, South Carolina, and was seized at the request of the British consul. Nash claimed he was an American citizen named Jonathan Robbins. Adams, with clear evidence he was not who he said he was, ordered him turned over to the British.

The Republicans used this as another excuse for attacking Adams. In the House, Livingston and several other representatives, all friends of Jefferson who wanted to do Adams damage, accused him of "dangerous interference" in judicial matters, despite the fact that the House had papers proving Nash was not Robbins. Livingston even proposed that Adams be censured. John Marshall, also a Representative in the House, was indignant at such blatant political maneuvering, and made a brilliant speech in Adams' defense. The measure was defeated.

Unfortunately, much of the Federalist press and many of the Federalists, in and out of government, were also causing Adams problems. Not the least of those doing him harm were the Federalists in his own Cabinet. Though he was not immediately aware of it, Pickering, McHenry, and Wolcott had formed a cabal to deny him a second term, and were actively seeking behind the scenes to have Chief Justice Oliver Ellsworth elected President.

Despite the efforts of some to keep the news from Adams, including Abigail, who was worried about her husband's health, it leaked through to him. By this time Adams had become increasingly wary of, and irritated by, Pickering, ever since he had delayed fulfilling his directive the previous October to prepare instructions for the peace mission. In fact, Adams had thought of removing Pickering from his Cabinet as early as November.

The many rumors and reports Adams had received since then about Pickering's disloyalty had only increased his desire to get rid of him. He was reluctant to act, however, for two reasons. The first was lack of positive proof of Pickering's disloyalty, and, since Adams was both a lawyer and a highly ethical man, this could very well be true. The second reason was, because it was an election year, Adams was afraid a change in his Cabinet might jeopardize his chances for reelection. Republican victories in several states that spring, especially the defeat of the Federalists in New York for the state legislature, which determined the appointment of electors for the coming national election, made it clear the election would be close.

At a dinner in the Presidential mansion on May 5, to which Secretary of War McHenry had been invited to discuss a minor appointment, Adams' frustration and anger, so long held in check, boiled over. He attacked the unsuspecting and surprised McHenry, charging him and Pickering and Wolcott of disloyalty and of being toadies of Hamilton. He then turned his rage on Hamilton, who wasn't present, saying he would rather serve as Vice-President under Jefferson than under Hamilton (a statement that got back to Hamilton and widened the rift between them). He fired McHenry on the spot, and the next day McHenry tendered his resignation. Four days later Adams asked for Pickering's resignation. This time, however, he did it by letter, avoiding direct confrontation for fear, perhaps, of once again losing his temper.

The shakeup in his Cabinet, though necessary, was something Adams later conceded he should have done earlier in his term of office. Now, with the election pending, the shake-up not only provided ammunition for the opposition to use against Adams, but it caused a split among the Federalists that would hinder his chances for reelection. Since it was almost the end of the congressional session and nothing could be done about the brouhaha at the moment, Abigail left for Quincy on May 17, while Adams stayed behind to clear up some remaining business.

The first such business was to disband the army that had been raised for the *faux* war with France. It was a most popular move and was swiftly accomplished by the Congress. A more difficult concern was what to do about John Fries and two other farmers from Eastern Pennsylvania who had been convicted of rebellion the previous year for stirring up resistance against payment of Federal taxes on private land. The three farmers had been condemned to death.

After studying the case, and against the advice of his entire Cabinet, Adams declared it a riot, not a rebellion, and pardoned the men. It turned out to be a popular move that helped, not hurt, him.

Then, since he would be the first person to occupy the Presidential mansion in the new Congressionally-created District of Columbia when Congress reconvened in the fall, he left Philadelphia at the end of the month to inspect the house and Capitol now nearing completion. (Though the Capitol was officially referred to as Federal City, many were already calling it "Washington" in honor of the first President.)

The city, however it was called, was hardly finished when Adams made his visit. It was without paved roads and had few private buildings, which consisted mainly of a few hotels and unfinished public buildings being reared among tree stumps in a barren landscape. Adams, however, wrote to Abigail that he liked what he saw and looked forward to occupying the new presidential mansion. (Because of its spanking new white paint job, it was already being called the "White House.")

While in the Capitol, he was feted at a dinner attended by seventy people who had already settled into boarding rooms, hotels, and the few private homes existent. He also dined with John Quincy's in-laws, the Johnson's, and with Attorney General Charles Lee and his family in their comfortable home across the Potomac River in Alexandria, Virginia.

After this brief visit, Adams left for Quincy early on June 14, hoping for a quiet, restful summer at Peacefield despite the campaign heating up. Though he tried to stay out of it, as he had in the previous campaign, it turned out to be exceedingly difficult. He found himself under attack not only from Jefferson and the Republicans, but from many Federalists as well. These included people he once considered friends, such as Francis Dana, his former secretary in Europe, and John Lowell, who had taken over his law practice after he left for Europe in 1777.

The most vicious attack, however, was reserved for Hamilton, who this time did it openly. At the end of October, a little more than a month before the electors were to meet on December 4, Hamilton published a 54-page pamphlet attacking Adams' character. In it he drudged up every known incident that showed Adams in a bad light, including his supposed jealousy and vanity and an "ungovernable temper" that, Hamilton claimed, sometimes made him act irrationally. Worse, by suggesting Adams was senile, the pamphlet went so far as to question his sanity.

It was perhaps the most damaging attack on Adams of the campaign. But it also had the damaging effect of pretty much ending Hamilton's career on the stage of national politics. He published it against the advice of many wiser heads, and the public eventually saw it for what it was, character assassination of a low order that did its writer dishonor. The major effect of the pamphlet was on the electors, elected or appointed in November, who would be called upon in December to cast their ballots for President.

At that time the electors did not have to strictly follow the wishes of their constituencies, but could exercise their own right to choose, and not all states provided for the electors to be elected by the public. In fact, only six states allowed for direct election, while the electors in the remaining states were appointed by the legislators of the state who, it was presumed, represented the wishes of their constituencies. In 1800, because of this peculiarity in "appointing" electors rather than their election by the public, indications of who would likely win the Presidency were perhaps clearer before the actual election than they are today (though today polls tell us much about the likelihood of which candidate would win).

The devastating losses of the Federalists to the Republicans in the state elections in New York a few months earlier was a clear indication the state would be lost to Adams. It was a state he had won in 1796, and it was pivotal to his reelection. All this, however, was still ahead of Adams when he left Quincy in the middle of October (Abigail, ill with rheumatism, was to follow a week later) to return to Washington for the new session of Congress.

He did not hear of the Hamilton pamphlet until the day after he moved into the White House, on November 1. Then, as bad as that was, there followed the disclosure of a letter Adams had written while Vice-President to Tenche Cox, an acquaintance in the Treasury, which further reduced his reelection chances.

The letter, written in 1792, concerned the appointment of Thomas Pinckney as ambassador to England. Adams, with ill-concealed bias, accused the Pinckneys of having made an attempt to get him (Adams) removed when he was ambassador, and suggested that strings were pulled in Britain to have Thomas appointed. It was an indiscretion that should have remained private, but it surfaced because Coxe had swung over to the Republican side and supplied the editor of the Republican *Aurora* with a copy.

It was especially embarrassing to Adams because Charles Cotesworth Pinckney, the brother of Thomas, was a Federalist running on the same ticket. Pinckney generously claimed the letter was a forgery. When that didn't work, he suggested that Adams disavow having written it. That wasn't possible, either. The best Adams could do was to say he had no memory of having written the letter. If he had, he said, he certainly would not have asserted that strings were pulled in Britain to get Thomas the job.

In addition to the mounting political difficulties during this month before the election, another sad event occurred that greatly distressed Adams. Abigail, on her way south from Quincy to join him in the White House, had stopped in New York to visit their son Charles, and found him deathly sick, his liver failing because of his alcoholism. Bloated and jaundiced, he was obviously dying. In fact, the doctor said he had only a few days, or weeks at most, to live. It was especially distressing to the Adamses because alcoholism at that time was considered a moral issue rather than a disease, and as parents they worried where they had gone wrong.

In addition to all the bad news, the Adamses had much else on their minds. One was settling into the huge barn of a house (it took thirteen fireplaces to keep it from being too drafty to live in) that was the Presidential mansion. It had a gorgeous view of the Potomac River from the mound on which it was built, but most of the land around it was still barren, and the house itself was largely unfurnished. Making it livable was something Abigail would have to achieve on her own, for John was kept busy with political matters and affairs of state.

Congress finally attained a quorum on November 22, and Adams, after a short ride down the wide, unpaved road that was to become Pennsylvania Avenue, delivered his Fourth annual address. It was a brief speech, for which the assembled congressman were most grateful, since it was a cold day and the room of the House in which they met was drafty and cold. The speech was brief because there was little for Adams to report. There was still no word from the peace commissioners he had sent to France, and the other major concern, the vote of the electors in the different states, wouldn't occur for another two weeks.

While Adams hoped to the very end that something would occur that would ensure his reelection, his defeat was pretty much a forgone conclusion. He knew he could not hope to win any votes in the South (as it turned out, he won four votes in South Carolina); and New York, which was pivotal to his reelection, was, he knew, already lost to him. He continued all his life to blame the loss on Hamilton's machinations, but in truth New York was lost to the Republicans mainly because of unpopular Federalist policies, among them direct taxes, what was considered their Anglophilia by the Republicans, and the Alien and Sedition Acts.

The electors assembled to vote in their various states on December 4, and after a few days the results began to trickle in. The first states to be heard from were Pennsylvania, Maryland, and New Jersey, with Adams and Pinckney each receiving nineteen votes, and Jefferson and Burr each receiving thirteen. A few days later Connecticut and Delaware were heard from; their twelve votes went to the Federalists. The tide began to turn when New York cast its twelve votes for the Republicans, and by the time Virginia and Massachusetts were heard from, Adams' lead had narrowed to one vote: he had forty-seven votes, Jefferson forty-six.

Adams knew it was the end, for it was mainly the South that remained to be heard from, and the South was expected to vote overwhelmingly Republican. The only question was whether Burr (the first man to run openly for the presidency), who was running a close second among the Republicans, or Jefferson would be president. The final tally, after the votes of Georgia and Tennessee arrived on December 23, showed Jefferson and Burr tied for first place with seventy-three votes each. Adams' total was sixty-five. The tie threw the election into the House of Representatives, where a decision wouldn't be made for some time.

While it was not the result Adams had wished for (he had hoped against hope until the very end), it was not unexpected, and he took it with some equanimity, despite personal feelings of rejection. Abigail, on the other hand, though distressed for her husband's sake, was pleased with the result. She looked forward to a return to Quincy and, she hoped, the serenity of family life. Her only regret was that they would not have sufficient fortune to enable her husband to devote his efforts to improving their farm and thus keep himself more occupied with its day-to-day supervision.

The ten weeks remaining in Adams' term before he would be obliged to turn over the reins of office on March 4 were busy ones. As always, it was important for him to be busy during times of adversity. For more than his recent defeat was on his mind. A few days before the electoral votes started trickling in, he learned of the death of his son Charles, on November 30. The cause of death was listed as "dropsy," but it was the failure of his liver due to his alcoholism that was the true cause.

Fortunately, not all the news was bad. In early November, too late to affect the election or appointment of electors on November 4, word arrived in the United States of the success of the peace mission Adams had sent to France. On October 3, at Montefiore, a château north of Paris, the French had signed a treaty of peace (Bonaparte dismissed the *faux* war as a family quarrel) with the United States. The U.S. ambassadors were feted with gifts, and toasts were drunk to "perpetual peace."

It was a signal victory for Adams, and might have affected the election if the news had arrived earlier. Even so, much tension remained. The "Convention of Mortefontaine," as the treaty was called, was not ratified by the Senate until February 3, and then only after much wrangling. The official count of the ballots cast for president by the electors of the various states did not occur until February 11. The tie threw the election into the House of Representatives, where it took thirty-six ballots and almost a week's time, before the decision was finally made in Jefferson's favor.

Meanwhile, Abigail began her journey back to Quincy on February 13, three weeks ahead of her husband, to ready Stonyfield, as Adams *now* called their farm, for his arrival. In the little time remaining to him in his administration, his principal task was to appoint a host of judges to fill an expanded judiciary the lame-duck Federalist Senate had created at his request.

The judiciary act they passed doubled the number of circuit courts to six, creating twenty-three new judgeships. It was an all-consuming task that, in the few short weeks remaining, required Adams to work until late at night reviewing the qualifications and selecting those to be appointed. Because of his preference for those adhering to Federalist principles, his appointments were castigated in the Republican press as "the Duke of Braintree's Midnight Judges."

One of Adam's last acts was to recall his son John Quincy from Berlin. Undoubtedly his most important decision during these last few months was to appoint John Marshall to be Chief Justice of the Supreme Court (he signed the commission on the last day of January 1800). It was, in fact, the second most important appointment of his career, the first being his nomination of George Washington in 1775, as a member of the Continental Congress, to lead the militias fighting the British outside Boston and form them into the army that was eventually to achieve independence.

The opportunity to appoint Marshall came about when Oliver Ellsworth, the Chief Justice appointed by Washington, resigned because of illness. Though Adams first offered the position to John Jay, Marshall, as it turned out, had the perfect mind and character to establish and strengthen the Supreme Court as the third of the triumvirate (the Executive and the Congress being the other two) to rule the country successfully. Most important was the fact that Marshall was a comparatively young man of 45, who in all likelihood would serve for many years (he served 34 years, as it turned out) and leave an indelible stamp on the federal judiciary.

As his presidency drew to a close, Adams was too busy to leave the White House. Indeed, he was still signing commissions to the judiciary on the eve of the inauguration. Despite that, the next day, March 4, 1800, he was up before dawn. Since no one had asked him to be present at Jefferson's inauguration, and he had no desire to be there, he left quietly at 4 A.M. by public carriage to join his beloved wife and family at Quincy.

He left behind to participate in the inauguration at noon three men who detested one another: Aaron Burr, an opportunist who had already been sworn in as Vice-President by the Senate, Thomas Jefferson, who was to be sworn in as President, and the newly-confirmed Chief Justice John Marshall, who was to swear Jefferson in, a man whom he detested, and who detested him.

Adams, though bitter at not being reelected and feeling rejected by the public he had so faithfully served, was happy to be out of it. Abigail, of course, was happier still.

Chapter Eleven
Quincy (1801-1826)

Adams' homecoming was as quiet as it could be. Mainly there was only Abigail waiting to welcome him home. And hardly had he shut the door behind him when there began one of the worst storms in local memory. It was a "nor'easter" from off the Atlantic with high winds and heavy rains that went on with no real let-up for the next ten days. It kept any potential visitors away, and Adams, locked in his study with time to do nothing but think, was clearly depressed.

First of all, he felt deeply the rejection, as he saw it, of the American people. He had no doubt it was caused by his decision to send the peace mission to France when everyone else was against it, especially the Federalists on whom he depended for political support. He blamed in particular the machinations of Alexander Hamilton, realizing at last that Hamilton had been out to undo him from the beginning – in short, for the previous ten years.

Adams also had the time now to at last grieve over the death of his son Charles, whose unrealized potential was destroyed by the disease that ultimately killed him. Alcoholism was to be a dreadful blight on the Adams family, passed on from Abigail's family (her brother William Smith had been an alcoholic) and persisting for many generations. It also destroyed their son Thomas Boylston and two of the sons of John Quincy, one of whom jumped, it is presumed, from the rear deck of a boat on its way from Boston to New York.

But perhaps the most significant indication that Adams was depressed during this period was that, normally an indefatigable letter writer, he wrote no letters for months after he arrived back in Quincy, and he rarely left the house, not even to go to Boston. Only better weather and work on the farm, and the gathering of friends and family, gradually brought him back to a more peaceful and sanguine frame of mind. Though he considered himself an old man (by the standards of the time he was), sans teeth, touched by palsy, with his energies declining, he still had twenty-five years more to live.

A bright spot in those early months was the return of John Quincy and Louisa from Europe (Adams had ordered their return from Berlin before he left office). They arrived in Philadelphia on September 4, 1801 with their first-born son, George Washington Adams. After a few days rest, Louisa went with the child to visit her parents in Washington while John Quincy proceeded to Quincy. Louisa finally rejoined her husband in Quincy in November.

She met her parents-in-law for the first time with considerable trepidation. Still sick with a cold, she knew the meeting did not go well. Normally vivacious and talkative in the right company, she was so nervous she felt distant and knew she must have appeared aloof. She was especially afraid of Abigail, quite aware of her high standards. From her point of view, the one bright spot was "the old man," John Adams himself, who immediately took to her, as she did to him.

Fortunately for her, they didn't stay long in Quincy. John Quincy returned to the law and, opening a practice in Boston, moved his family there. It was assumed he had given up all thought of politics, but he had hardly begun his practice when he was appointed to the Great and General Court, and soon after that ran for Congress from Boston. He was soundly beaten by his Republican opponent, but the next year was appointed to a vacant seat in the Senate by the Massachusetts legislature, beating out Timothy Pickering for that great honor.

Despite his busyness, John Quincy was able to visit his parents most weekends, and saw his father's spirits revive. One of the things he did to help his father recover was to encourage him to write his autobiography. Adams began work on it in 1804, and continued writing intermittently on it for the next several years. He also began letter writing again, and plunged heavily into reading. These activities, plus the presence of his grandchildren and other family members, and his arduous work on the farm helping the hired hands, resulted in the depression gradually lifting.

Along with this lifting of his spirits came a revived interest, not only in his own political past, but in the political issues of the day. His opinions were expressed mostly in correspondence with old friends, especially with Dr. Benjamin Rush of Philadelphia, one of the foremost physicians of his time.

In addition to his practice, Rush lectured and published treatises on public health issues. Many of his ideas were advanced and controversial for his day. He had also been a participant in the Continental Congresses, was one of the signers of the Declaration of Independence, and he and Adams had been good friends in those days, even though Rush was a Republican.

Adams initiated the correspondence in February of 1804, and it went on until Rush's death 10 years later. It enabled both men, each of whom felt like odd man out in these later years, to cover a wide range of topics, from old friends, to politics old and new, to their thoughts and opinions on almost every conceivable subject of interest to them. The correspondence contributed greatly to Adams' feeling of well-being and happiness, for it helped him satisfy his two great passions after the family and the farm: reading and writing.

Not all was serene, however, in this early period of his retirement. In 1805 he received an unexpected attack from someone whose family and his had always been friends. In that year Mercy Otis Warren, undoubtedly the foremost female intellectual of her day, published her two-volume *History of the Rise, Progress, and Termination of the American Revolution.*

It wasn't the first history of the Revolution that had been published, but she was a well-known writer whose previous publications, most notably plays and poems, strongly supported the new American Republic and were popular. Also, her credentials were impeccable, for she was the wife of James Warren, a distinguished politician of Massachusetts who had long been active in the revolutionary cause, and a member of the politically active Otis family.

She was a friend of Thomas Jefferson as well as the Adamses, but inclined toward Jefferson's political philosophy. Much influenced by the anti-Federalists, she portrayed Adams as someone who had been corrupted by the courts of Europe and therefore had monarchist leanings. She considered Adams's political views a betrayal of the American revolutionary ideals that had led to the founding of the nation. And on a more personal level she wrote that Adams was one whose passions and prejudices often overruled his sagacity.

Needless to say, Adams, ever sensitive about his reputation, especially how he would be viewed by history, took it personally. Incensed, he wrote a series of indignant letters to Warren, calling her to task for all the misrepresentations, as he considered them, in her *History*. "What have I done, Mrs. Warren," he wrote in his first letter to her, "to merit so much malevolence from a lady concerning whom I never in my life uttered an unkind word or disrespectful insinuation." She responded to his first few letters, trying to soothe his ruffled feelings, but he went on to write ten in all, trying to set the record straight, before giving up.

By this time Adams had also pretty much given up on his intermittent efforts to write his autobiography. He excused himself by saying that it would be seen as too self-serving. This despite his many letters and a series of articles in the Boston *Patriot* defending the reputation of his administration and himself and his thoughts on government. The truth was, while a prolific writer, he never took much care with his writing, and it tended to be overlong and disorderly. The autobiography was especially distasteful to him because it involved rummaging through old letters and papers.

Correspondence was easier, because he was free to express himself without giving thought to the possible consequences of his letters. He was especially grateful to have an old friend like Rush to whom he could fulminate without worrying that his comments would be taken the wrong way or, far worse, be passed on and possibly find publication. When Jefferson's Presidency ended, for example, Adams wrote, knowing he could trust Rush: "How he will get rid of his remorse in his retirement, I do not know. He must know that he leaves the government infinitely worse than he found it, and that from his own error and ignorance."

Another theme running through the correspondence of Rush and Adams is concern about the history of the Revolution and their place in it. They especially worried what yet-to-be-written histories would reveal to future generations. At one point Rush even laments the wasted time, as he saw it, that that history had cost him. In a letter dated April 22, 1807 he writes: "In looking back upon the years of our Revolution, I often wish [I now had] those ten thousand hours that I wasted in public pursuits and that I now see did no permanent work [good] for my family nor my country." Adams, always more sanguine, disagreed.

What Adams was *not* sanguine about was his own place in that history. As early as April 4, 1790, long before their regular correspondence began, he wrote to Rush that: "The history of our Revolution will be one continued lie from one end to the other. The essence of the whole will be that Dr. Franklin's electrical rod smote the earth and out sprang General Washington. That Franklin electrified him with his rod – and thenceforward these two conducted all the policies, negotiations, legislatures and war."

Rush was, of course, not the only one Adams corresponded with over the years. Rush was a friend of both Adams and Jefferson, and was finally able to renew the friendship between them. Again, it was Adams who initiated the correspondence, in 1808. Jefferson, however, willingly responded, grateful to renew the friendship they had had when they both were serving overseas during and after the war.

Jefferson was especially fond of Abigail, and they, too, had corresponded before. When his daughter Polly died, for instance, Abigail wrote him a note of condolence. She was especially distressed because Polly was the young girl she had taken under her wing when Polly first arrived in London, along with the slave girl Sally Hemings, herself only fifteen or sixteen according to Abigail (she was actually 14), before going on to join her father in Paris.

The correspondence between John Adams and Thomas Jefferson was very satisfying to them both, and it lasted until a few weeks before their simultaneous deaths in 1826. Adams, especially, needed the opportunity to vent his thinking on a wide range of subjects. Both men were heavy readers and interested in history, science, and the arts, as well as farming and politics.

Jefferson was one of the few men of his times whose interests ranged as widely as Adams' did, and who had the intellect that made it possible to share those interests. Both men, considerably mellowed, gained much from the exchange in the way of personal growth also, especially in forgiving wrongs and admitting errors.

Adams was too prolific a writer to be satisfied merely with personal correspondence, however copious his letters (he wrote twice as many letters to Jefferson as Jefferson wrote to him, for example). Although Adams perhaps never admitted it to himself, he longed for a more public venue.

The opportunity arose in 1814 when John Taylor of Caroline published *An Inquiry into the Principles and Policy of the Government of the United States,* in which he attacked Adams' *A Defence of the Constitutions of Governments of the United States of America,* written in 1787 while Adam was still in England. Taylor's basic thesis was that Adams' political thinking was pre-Revolutionary and, therefore, out-of-date. Adams, he claimed, thought in terms, still, of monarchy, aristocracy, the elite, the common folk, and other such notions that weren't compatible with the post-Revolutionary realities of a democratic nation.

Rising to the bait, Adams wrote a series of thirty-two letters over the next two years defending his political theories, which were published in a Boston newspaper. His theories of government, at least as they applied to the state and federal constitutions of the nation then being born, had always been consistent. Always the realist where human nature was concerned, he was a forceful advocate of the separation of powers, of a system of checks and balances, an independent judiciary, and a bicameral legislature.

After America's independence from Great Britain was declared in July of 1776, the colonies were advised to create new constitutions and set up state governments. Many wrote to John Adams for advice because of a long letter he wrote at one colony's request. To satisfy the many requests, Adams enlarged the letter and had it published as a pamphlet he titled *Thoughts on Government.* In it he advocated the kind of government he had always thought best for both the states and the nation. It was the kind of government the states and nation finally adopted, and, of course, with the addition of the Bill of Rights and many subsequent amendments, is the constitution we have today.

Adams also wrote the constitution for his own state of Massachusetts which, slightly amended, is the constitution that exists today. It is thus no hyperbole to call Adams the "architect" of America's freedom, especially if we remember that copies of his *Defence* of the States' constitutions, published in London in March of 1787 and written with the ostensible purpose of influencing the European governments to understand and favor the new nation, reached America in time to influence the delegates to the Constitutional Convention held later that year in Philadelphia.

In March of 1809, the Adamses received the news that one of the first things President James Madison had done upon assuming office was to appoint John Quincy to be ambassador to Russia. John received the news with mixed emotions, pleased with the recognition given his son, seeing it as a reflection of his own vindication as

President. At the same time, he was saddened by the possibility that he might never see his son and his family again, a view shared by Abigail, who ardently desired her family about them in their old age. She felt that, as a family, they had already sacrificed enough for their country.

Initially the Senate rejected John Quincy's nomination, and his parents were relieved. But the Senate finally gave in under pressure from the new administration and approved it. Thus it was with sad hearts that both Abigail and John watched John Quincy and Louisa depart for that far-off country of snow and ice.

One consolation for John was the conviction that his son's appointment was an important mission. Russia, he wrote, was "a tremendous power whose future influence cannot be foreseen." Another consolation for him, which was Abigail's *only* consolation, was that the departing pair left their children, George Washington and the newly born Charles Francis, at Quincy with them.

In addition to the many appointments President James Madison would have to make, he would soon have to face another problem. It was a problem Adams had long foreseen: war with Britain. British boarding of American vessels at sea to impress U.S. citizens into their navy had gotten worse (their excuse was that they were seeking deserters from their own navy), as had their interference with American shipping and commerce with other nations, in particular with France. There were also clashes in the West between American frontiersmen and British soldiers and their Indian allies over land.

It had gotten worse, in Adams' view, because of the disastrous policy of Jefferson during his two administrations of reducing the Navy Adams had so sedulously begun to a mere handful of gunboats that could hardly do more than guard their own ports. Fortunately, in Adams' view, Madison was not so unwise. He gradually built up the Navy so that when war was declared on June 18, 1812 the United States had the ability to inflict serious damage on British warships.

Most notable were the early victories of Stephen Decatur and Isaac Hull, commander of the *Constitution*. But the decisive victory of Captain Oliver Perry over the British Navy on Lake Erie in September of that year was the most hopeful sign that the Americans would prevail. This hope was not destroyed by the British bombardment of Washington, DC, in August of 1814. Victories on land, most notably at Thames, Plattsburgh, and Fort McHenry finally convinced the British to enter serious negotiations for peace.

The Treaty of Ghent ending the war, though it did not settle any of the major issues between the combatants, was signed on Dec. 24, 1814.[4] Except for the British bombardment of the nation's capital, with its attendant fires, the United States came out of the conflict relatively unscathed.

The war was the last of any conflict between the two nations. There was a time of uncertainty during the U.S. Civil War, when it was feared that the British might enter the conflict on the side of the South. But that situation was eased by another Adams, Charles Francis Adams, son of John Quincy. And by the next century the two countries were allies in two of the most terrible conflicts of all time, World Wars I and II.

The two years immediately following the War of 1812 were difficult ones for Abigail and John Adams. Their daughter Nabby had had one of her breasts painfully removed, without the use of anesthesia (this was often the case in 1811, as whiskey, rum, and other hard liquor was about the only pain-killer they had). Unfortunately,

---

4   *An interesting sidelight of this history is the decisive victory of Andrew Jackson and his troops at the battle for New Orleans, which took place on Jan. 14, 1815, after the treaty had been signed.*

the cancer recurred in 1813, and she returned home to die. Her death took place only three weeks later.

After that it seemed to John, who had been seriously ill that winter and into the spring of 1814, that death was all about him as, one after the other, most of their old friends died. In 1815 the last of Abigail' sisters, Eliza Peabody, died. After that their old friend Cotton Tufts, who had managed their affairs when they were stationed in Europe, died. Then, a few months later, in December of that year, their son-in-law William Smith, also died.

The next year, however, things began to look brighter. In November they learned that John Quincy was being recalled to become Secretary of State in the administration of James Monroe, who would be sworn in as President on March 4, 1817. The thought of their son and his family returning to the United States lightened the thoughts of Abigail and John considerably.

Though Abigail was sick most of that winter, by spring she had recovered so well that John declared his wife "restored to her characteristic vivacity, activity, wit, sense, and benevolence." With her health restored, she became the wife and companion, mother and grandmother, she had always been.

At the time John Quincy was recalled, he was on a special mission to England, and had left Louisa in St. Petersburg with the children. She rejoined him in England after a harrowing trip across Europe in the dead of winter in a sleigh with the children. And when John Quincy's duties were concluded late that spring, they at last set sail for the United States.

They arrived in Boston in August, but had little time for a homecoming. President Monroe was waiting for John Quincy to assume his duties as Secretary of State, and they set off almost immediately for Washington and all the hassles of duty. Fortunately for John and Abigail, John Quincy and Louisa left their school-age children behind, which cheered them considerably.

Though they didn't speak of it beyond the family, they were also cheered by the thought that since Madison, Jefferson's Secretary of State, had succeeded *him* as President; and Monroe, Madison's Secretary of State had succeeded *him* as President, might it not be John Quincy's turn to be President next? So it turned out to be. Unfortunately, Abigail did not live to see it.

John and the family had expected Abigail to outlive him, since she was so much younger than he. But she took sick again in October of the following year; and this time is was serious. She was diagnosed as having typhoid fever, and heavily dosed with quinine. Since she was 74 years old, the family knew there was little hope she would survive. On the morning of October 26, 1818, she recovered enough to tell John she was dying. She died two days later, October 28, at one o'clock in the afternoon.

She was buried in a special vault in Quincy on November 1, with many family members and luminaries in attendance. It was expected John would soon join her and be buried in the same crypt across the road from the little white church in Quincy. He, however, was to outlive her by another eight years, living to what would be considered at any time a ripe old age.

It was not a happy time for him. Though eventually, with the help of the many grandchildren and other family members who lived with him, he managed slowly to recover his spirits and find the will to live. As he wrote to an old friend, Charles Carroll, in July of 1820: "I enjoy life and have as good a spirit as I ever had, but my fabric has become very weak, almost worn out."

Those living in the same house included his son Thomas Boylston and his family. Though educated as a lawyer, Thomas was an alcoholic like his brother Charles and had never been able to adequately support his family. It was decided there wasn't enough room for Thomas and his family in the house at Peacefield, undoubtedly because of his condition. But maybe not, for fourteen people, including two servants, were already living there.

Thomas and his family moved into the original house in Braintree, where they lived rent free as "caretakers," courtesy of John Quincy, who had purchased the house from his father after John lost all his money in a bad investment John Quincy himself had recommended. The house was not too far from Peacefield, and Thomas' five children and their mother (Thomas had married Ann Harrod of Haverhilll, MA, in 1805) often ate their meals there.

Thomas himself was drinking heavily, and was largely unemployed and unemployable. His nephew Charles Francis characterized him as a "brute." John, who had had the painful experience of not being able to do much to curb Charles' drinking, pretty much left Thomas alone. Even so, Thomas managed to outlive his father by six years, dying in 1832 at the age of sixty.

Among the pleasant things that happened in these last years was a visit from Hannah Quincy, the girl to whom in his youth he would have proposed but for the unexpected entrance of some friends at the last minute that "saved" him. Though neither he nor Hannah left any record of what went on at that meeting, Josiah Quincy, a young Harvard student employed during the summers to assist the ex-President with his correspondence, did.

Josiah wrote in his diary that Adams greeted Hannah with: "What! Madam! Shall we not go walk in Cupid's Grove together?" She seemed, he wrote, momentarily embarrassed, but recovered quickly enough to reply, "Ah, sir, it would not be the first time."

They were then both almost 91.

John also sat for two portraits and a bust made from a plaster cast of his head in his later years. He seemed to enjoy the experience, though Jefferson, who had had the same thing done, found it almost unbearable. The best painting by far, he and the family agreed, was by Gilbert Stuart, who was almost as old as John himself at the time (both nearing eighty), about 1815.

The family thought the painting[5] had a certain vibrancy that brought out Adams' inner spirit. The head that resulted from the plaster cast, on the other hand, made Adams look like a sour old man, and mean-spirited. But to some who knew him, they seemed to express the two sides of Adam's character.

In addition to the sculpting and painting (John enjoyed talking to the artists), a corps of 200 West Point cadets marched out from Boston one day to serenade him. Adams watched from the front porch while they played and sang a song written especially for the occasion called "Adams and Liberty." John thoroughly enjoyed it, and afterwards shook the hand of each of the cadets and said a word to each of them as they approached him on the porch.

Adams was also at this time invited to be a member of a Board that was being convened to revise the Massachusetts Constitution that John had largely written. He was even asked to chair the sessions, but he declined because of the feebleness of age. He did manage, however, to attend two of the sessions of the Board during the two months of winter when it met, when the winter weather and his own energies permitted.

The only time he spoke was to propose an amendment guaranteeing freedom of religion to all citizens in the State of Massachusetts. But he could barely make himself heard in the hubbub of Faneuil

---

5   *This is the painting, originally done circa 1815, when John was nearing 80, as redone by Gilbert Stuart Newton, which appears on the cover of this book.*

Hall, and the amendment did not garner the necessary number of votes to pass. And since no one else picked up the cudgels for the proposed amendment, and because Adams lacked the vigor to pursue the matter, it was dropped.

Adams thought it "imbecilic" of him to have attended, when a more energetic younger person might have been more useful to the convention. In the end the constitution he had created survived, with but a few amendments. His only disappointment, he said, was in not having been vigorous enough to achieve his goal that government should impose no religious restrictions on its citizens. Despite the inclusion of the word "Christian" in the document as a requirement of citizenship, however, Massachusetts, has never imposed it on anyone living in the State.

Adams himself had come a long way from the Puritan faith of his ancestors. Unable to subscribe to the tenets of that religion, which prevented him, as you may remember, from becoming the minister his father had hoped he might be, he became more and more liberal as he grew older as far as religion was concerned.

Over a lifetime he had never tired of reading about religion, but in the end he couldn't accept the Christian ideas of the trinity, the ascension and divinity of Jesus, and much else. His beliefs near the end of his life were very close to those the Unitarians professed. And, indeed, that is in effect what he had become.

John Quincy had once intimated to his father that he would like to write his biography after his death. The idea attracted John, since he knew his son would give him a fair hearing. He was also concerned that many of those engaged in the Revolution and the establishment of the Republic were not being sufficiently recognized (James Otis, for one), and he hoped his son would rectify that by including their names and deeds in the book.

To make the job easier for his son, he spent much of his time in these later years seeking and assembling his papers, such as diary entries, ledgers, and the copious notes he had made on so many occasions. But the most onerous task by far, a task he never quite finished, was sorting out the enormous correspondence he had carried on over the years with so many different people.

One reason was that much of his time was taken up by the parade of people wishing to meet him during these years. He was even honored by a visit from President Madison and his wife, Dolly. Though he tried to be gracious to all, the visits that pleased him the most were by his own children and grandchildren.

Especially agreeable to him was a visit from his granddaughter Caroline (daughter of Nabby and William Smith) and her husband and their young daughter. The family was dear to him, and the children knew it. Even John Quincy, though Secretary of State, managed to visit his father each summer, along with Louisa.

Louisa through the years had been a faithful correspondent, sometimes writing on a daily basis to give Adams the news of what was going on in Washington, or simply to share her views with him. He thoroughly enjoyed her letters and kept up his letters to her during his declining years. In addition, he remained a voluminous reader, despite complaining of what he called his "dim eyes."

Reading, he commented in 1818, some years earlier, is what "has kept me alive." By the time he was 85, however, his eyesight was so bad he had to ask others to read to him. But perhaps because he lacked the mental strength to lift the heavier tomes of philosophy and the classics, or perhaps out of consideration for his readers, he turned toward lighter reading, such as the novels of Sir Walter Scott and James Fenimore Cooper.

He remained mentally alert to the very end, though his palsy (he called it "quiversation") continued to get worse. Eventually the shaking of his hands got so bad he could no longer write, either, and he had to have help in that area, too. You can tell these later letters were scribed by others because they are filled with misspellings and poor grammar, something Adams would not have permitted if he had been doing it himself.

Letter writing was so important to him (it was his chief contact with the outside world, and a major intellectual stimulant) that he kept it up as best he could. Even his correspondence with Jefferson, though they were both sick, was maintained until two weeks before their deaths. At the end, in his 91st year, Adams could do no more, and his infirmities took over.

Death came fairly quickly after a slow decline in his physical capacities over the past several years. His rheumatism bothered him more, and he could no longer ride his horse about the farm as he once did, or even take the walks he once liked. But the failing eyesight and increasing fatigue were the results of aging rather than of disease or ill-health.

The truth was, he was remarkably healthy for a man of his age, and it was fortunate his mental faculties remained as acute as they did. He still loved life, whether it was conversing with the many visitors and members of his family who lived with him, or "rambling" in the garden, or simply staring out the window at the glittering results of an ice storm during the night.

He was fortunate, too, in living long enough to see his son John Quincy elected President in 1825. The election was close. Neither John Quincy nor Andrew Jackson, the man he ran against, had a majority of the electoral votes (Jackson had more of the popular vote), and the contest, like that of Jefferson and Aaron Burr, had to be decided in the House of Representatives.

Again it was close, with the House divided. Henry Clay, a powerful politician of his day who favored John Quincy, happened to be Speaker of the House on February 9, 1825 when the deciding votes were cast, and John Quincy won. When the news reached Peacefield five days later, there were many congratulatory letters, including one from Jefferson praising his son and lauding his election, and expressing words honoring the father.

The transfer of power took place, as it did in those days because of the difficulties of communication and travel, on March 4. John Marshall, who had been appointed Chief Justice of the Supreme Court by John Adams, presided over the ceremony. John was too feeble to make the arduous journey to attend, but just the news of it seemed to revive his spirits and his energies.

Though short of breath, his mind was good and he could talk at length. And though he didn't expect to see his son again, since John Quincy would be so busy in Washington, he continued in good health through the remainder of the year. In the fall of 1824 John Quincy did, however, manage to spend a few days with him, which again revived Adams spirits, if not his energy.

He was at that time nearing his 90th birthday, in October of 1825, and he continued on in reasonably good health through most of the next spring. As the time for the 50th anniversary of the founding of the nation approached, Adams began to receive invitations to attend various celebrations, as did Jefferson. They both had to decline, knowing full well they did not have the energy to travel or participate in any such festivities.

The last appeal to Adams was made by local townspeople at the end of June 1826, a few days before the ceremonies were to be held in Quincy. Again, John had to decline because of feebleness. The dignitary sent to appeal to him, frustrated, asked if Adams would at least say a few words that some else could take down and deliver for him at the ceremonies in Quincy.

"Independence forever!" Adams responded.

The visitor asked Adams if he could add a few words.

"Not a word," Adams replied.

Jefferson and Adams were both quite ill as the anniversary approached. But each had the desire and the will to survive until the Fourth. On July 2, Jefferson lapsed into a coma, and his physician did not expect him to survive until the Fourth. At seven in the evening of the next day, he woke and asked if it was the Fourth. He lapsed back into his coma, and at four the next morning again woke and asked if it was the Fourth. He then lapsed into a coma, and died, without recovering, at one o'clock that afternoon, July 4.

Adams, who was still alive at that moment, heard the roar of the cannon in Quincy that was part of the celebration being held. It was, he said, music to his ears, before falling asleep again. A few hours later, he whispered, "Jefferson survives." At a little after six o'clock on that same day, his heart stopped beating.

The fact that both men, the only two signers of the Declaration of Independence still alive, died on the same day, the 50th anniversary of the day the Declaration was signed, stunned the nation. Newspapers headlined the story, and the nation was in awe, as if it were a divine omen.

Thomas Jefferson was buried in Monticello, John Adams in the vault beside his beloved wife Abigail, on July 7. The family had declined a public ceremony in Boston at public expense, but even so, there was an estimated crowd of 4,000 mourners in attendance before the small church and the graveyard across the road.

The news of Adams' death was late reaching John Quincy in Washington, and it wasn't until the 9th that he was able to begin the journey home. He arrived in Quincy on Sunday the 13th and only then, he said, standing in his father's study, did the gravity of what had happened sink in. For the first time he felt the great loss of his parents, both Abigail and John. The house was still at last.

John Quincy served only one term as President, but reentered politics by being elected, and reelected eight times, to the House of Representatives from Massachusetts. It has been said by some that he did more good for the nation as Representative than he had as President. He will also be remembered as the lawyer who defended the slaves on the *Amistad,* a Spanish ship that had foundered on coast of the United States, and won their right to be free.

True to his word to his father, he began, toward the close of his life, the biography he had promised to write. He completed only the first 100 pages, however. The remainder of the long, two-volume biography was completed by his son, Charles Francis Adams, who had served so notably as ambassador to Great Britain during the Civil War (the dreaded war that John Adams had foreseen at the founding of the nation).

The biography was first published in 1871 and, as intended, did much to restore the reputation of the second President of the United States. Since then his stature has seemed only to grow, and his sterling qualities of honesty, integrity, and perseverance are properly esteemed. In any age they are rare.

John Adams had them in abundance.

The Genius of the Founders

The United States in its founding was particularly blessed by the fact that the brightest and best talent, both men and women, rose to the cause and served in the Continental Congresses, the Army, and in overseas posts. The women served mainly on the home front by maintaining the farms and businesses while their husbands were engaged in the war separating the colonies from Great Britain and in establishing the government of a new nation such had never been seen before.

There were, of course, women like Mercy Otis Warren who wrote for the cause, and women who went with the troops, and joined their husbands overseas. Abigail Adams is among the brightest and best of these women. We were also fortunate that so many of the men and women who rallied to the cause were intellectuals, and that so many were free thinkers as far as religion was concerned. I'd like to close this brief biography by commenting upon five of the most prominent founders.

George Washington was not among those so intellectually blessed. He barely had the equivalent of a grade school education. And he was not even a great general. He rarely, if ever, spoke of

God, always referring to Providence to indicate a higher power. But George Washington had qualities that were absolutely essential for the founding of this nation. Among them were courage, perseverance, steadfastness, loyalty, dignity and great restraint of tongue and pen, though his anger could sometimes erupt in private situations. It helped, also, that he was tall and imposing, that he was willing to listen to counsel, and that he rarely took sides in factional disputes.

He also had a knack for surrounding himself with the best men and utilizing their talents. Two of his greatest generals, at least in the early stages of the War for Independence were civilians who learned the military arts through reading. These were Henry Knox and Nathaniel Greene, both of whom were from Boston, and both recruited by Washington at the very beginning of the war.

One was a bookseller, and the other was a foundry man. Washington was smart enough to listen to them and utilize their skills. They kept him, for example, from foolishly attacking the British when they occupied Boston, and from attacking New York City, which became an obsession with him, since it was there he suffered his most humiliating defeat.

Washington's own military experience was as a major assisting the British in their war against the French and Indians, and his only battle experience of any consequence was attacking the French at Fort Duquesne and suffering a humiliating defeat. Under the tutelage of Knox and Greene, he learned to fight a war of attrition, which was not his style. And he learned how to be patient, though he knew that in war daring is often called for, and the raid at Trenton was all of that..

On the intellectual side, Washington utilized the brains of Alexander Hamilton as aide-de-camp throughout the war, not only for writing most of his dispatches and letters, but also for advice.

Fortunately for him, Hamilton was a quick study and learned much about war strategy and tactics. Washington used this gift of surrounding himself with good men when it came to forming his Cabinet for his terms as President.

When it came time to retire, he amazed the world by his willingness to give up power. He was also smart enough to have James Madison write his Farewell Address, with minor help from Alexander Hamilton. This speech was not spoken, but published in a Philadelphia newspaper.

Alexander Hamilton was probably the most gifted man intellectually of all those who helped found this nation. He came from nothing, the bastard son of a Scotch man in the Caribbean, but his gifts were extraordinary. As a clerk in a store, he so impressed those he worked for that they made it possible for him to emigrate to the mainland and attend Kings College in New York. It seemed he could master any subject.

He studied the military and left school to join Washington's staff. After the war he became a lawyer and entered politics, which he soon also mastered. He turned to finance and became the first Secretary of the Treasury under Washington. It was as Treasurer that he perhaps made the greatest contribution to the new nation. He was for a strong federal government, and began his office by pressuring for the assumption of the States' war debts. He established the first national bank, issued sound money, and put the nation on a fiscally responsible basis, without which it would never have succeeded.

Unfortunately, he didn't have the moral standards required for a public figure. His adulterous relationship with a married woman scandalized the nation. While he was superb at politics, his lack of ethics got him into trouble there, too. His vicious attack on Adams when Adams was running for a second term ended Hamilton's political career. He should have known better, for he did it against the advice of his best friends, including James Madison.

In the end, his arrogance and pride brought him into a duel with Aaron Burr that ended his life and the enormous possibilities the future held for a man with his talents.

As far as his religious beliefs were concerned, Hamilton blew hot and cold. He was religiously fervid as a youth on St. Croix, and even wrote a poem on the ascension of the soul to heaven. At Kings College in New York he was known for his religiosity. But this soon vanished during the revolutionary years when he served with Washington.

In fact, Washington, who thought of him as a bit of a "rake," was surprised when it was announced that Hamilton was marrying the pious Elizabeth Schulyer from an old, established New York family. Elizabeth belonged to the Dutch Reform Church, but Hamilton himself never formally joined any church. At the end of his life, especially as he lay dying from the wound inflicted by Aaron Burr, he turned religious again and asked for the last rites that were part of his Episcopalian up-bringing.

Benjamin Franklin was also highly intellectual, though his ideas were of a more practical bent, given much to science and philosophizing upon life. Largely self-taught, his versatility was amazing. He learned the printing trade working for his brother in Boston, but soon left to set up his own shop in Philadelphia.

As he prospered, he began publishing newspapers and books, most notably *Poor Richard's Almanac,* which he, of course, wrote himself; it found a wide audience and is still available in book form to this day. As his interests grew, he helped start a public library, a fire department, a postal system, organize a militia, and much else, in Philadelphia.

Of his many scientific experiments, the most famous is perhaps flying a kite with a key on it to determine that lightning was indeed electricity. In France, where he spent sixteen of the last eighteen years of his life (leaving his wife at home in Philadelphia to manage their affairs), he was honored more as a scientist than anything else. Even as he was returning home from Europe at the end of his long service abroad, he took samples from the ocean to determine the make-up of the Gulf Stream. In short, he had an endless curiosity about nature, life, and people.

His knowledge of people showed a great wisdom, and though his style of socializing and mediation irked John Adams, who was more blunt and tactless, Franklin was undoubtedly one of the ablest diplomats this country has ever had. There is no doubt that it is due mainly to his polished and smooth diplomacy that France contributed so much to the colonies' efforts to throw off the restraints of British rule.

Above all, Franklin was pragmatic, and when necessary, he was shrewd enough to abandon protocol, as he did in joining Adams and Jay to make a separate peace with Great Britain, a peace that was far more advantageous to the newly formed nation than it might ever have been if the French were involved.

As far as Franklin's religious beliefs are concerned, he never willingly set foot in a church after he reached adulthood. But he was smart enough to countenance the religious beliefs of others, and keep his religious views, if any, to himself.

Thomas Jefferson, of course, was not only an intellectual, but a scholar, second to John Adams, perhaps, in his quest for knowledge. And his interests were certainly more wide-spread than those of Adams. They included, most notably, architecture and education, as well as classical learning.

Jefferson was more of a loner than Adams, and certainly had more time for reading and scholarship than did Adams with his large and extended family and duties. He also had more of an aptitude for the arts, and certainly for invention, of which Adams had none. He designed and built Monticello, invented things like a dumbwaiter to serve from the kitchen below to the dining room above. He also designed and founded the University of Virginia, of which he was most proud.

Jefferson was also a fine writer, which Adams most certainly was not. It was because of his reputation as a writer that he was assigned to the committee of five, of which Adams and Franklin were members, to draft the Declaration of Independence. The other members of the committee, aware of his skills, were happy to let him write the first draft, and saw little need to change anything in it, except for maybe a word or two.

Having written the Declaration of Indepence is perhaps what Jefferson is most remembered for today, more so than his Presidency or his ambassadorship to France. Adams always remained a bit envious of the fame the Declaration brought Jefferson, having himself thought it a rather minor task at the time.

Jefferson, of course, did not have, and except for Washington nor did few others, the integrity of Adams. He disliked confrontation and would use back-handed (devious) ways to attain his objectives. Another way to say this is that he was a coward. As Governor of Virginia he fled when British troops got too near, first at Richmond, and then at Monticello, to which he had fled.

Ambitious, as were all the Founding Fathers, he dropped out of Washington's Cabinet his second term to supposedly "retire" to Monticello. In fact he was planning to run for the Presidency and kept up with everything political that was going on, working through

Madison to pressure and move events in his direction. When he finally did run against Adams after Adams' first term, he paid a scurrilous journalist named James Callender to write scandalous articles about Adams for the newspapers of his day.

Eventually, Jefferson got his come-uppance. In time, when Callender felt Jefferson was not paying him enough to keep his mouth shut, he turned his scurrilous pen against his benefactor. As a side note: It is obvious Callender was an alcoholic. He died a drunkard's death, drowning in shallow water up to his knees.

John Adams was perhaps the most honest and plain-speaking of all the founders we have discussed. His integrity was of the highest, and this served the nation well in almost all the positions in which he served. For example, as a one-man Board of Ordinance during the early years of the Revolution, handling the requisition of supplies, he was scrupulously honest.

Which is not to say that others, like Richard Morris, who was wealthy to begin with and used much of his own money to supply the troops, was not. But, somehow, Morris managed to increase his wealth greatly during the war. Adams, on the other hand, left public service after a life-time of endeavor pretty much a poor man, except for the acquisition of some property and some small savings, which might be credited to Abigail's efforts.

Adams had, also, one quality that not everyone else had, a capacity for long and arduous work, day in and day out, month after month. Hard work brought him to a state of collapse when he was young and riding the circuit as a lawyer. And, again, when he was minister to The Netherlands and trying to get loans and recognition from the Dutch to pay the troops and make it possible to see the Revolutionary War through to a successful conclusion.

Adams had not an imposing presence like Jefferson and Washington, who were both unusually tall for the times. In fact, Adams was rather short and stout; "flubsy," in fact, is an old word, now outdated, that perfectly describes him. He could also be tactless on occasion. But he was a good orator, who could marshal his facts and speak at length to persuade others and attain his ends, which were always those of the nation succeeding in establishing and strengthening itself, when otherwise it might have failed.

As regards religion, you pretty much know Adams' story. He came from Puritan (Calvinist) stock, but found, when the time came to study for the ministry, he could not accept many of the Christian doctrines as they were taught at that time. For which reason, he gave up the pursuit of a career as a preacher, and became instead a lawyer. While he and Abigail always enjoyed attending church when they could, and listening to the sermons, his religious beliefs became more and more liberal over the years, and he himself more tolerant of the beliefs of others.

As you have read, his last public effort was to have the word "Christian" stricken from the Massachusetts constitution as a requirement for citizenship. Religion, he felt strongly, should never be a prerequisite for citizenship in any nation, especially the state of Massachusetts, and the United States of America.

At the end of his life, Adams had in fact become a Unitarian, if he was anything. That is, he was free to be a humanist, a theist, a deist, agnostic or atheist, or to have no beliefs at all. We owe our religious freedom today to the tolerant beliefs, or lack of belief, of our Founders.

It might be said that the founding of this nation was divinely-inspired. And it may have well been so. But what we *do* know is that we were blessed in having among the founders of this nation men who were blessed with both intellect and religious tolerance.

Chronology for the Life and Times of John Adams

1735   October 30 (Oct. 19, O.S.). John Adams born in North Precinct of Braintree, Mass

1740   Begins grade school education at Mrs. Belcher's; soon switches to Joseph Cleverly's school, in Braintree.

1744   King George's War between England and France begins November 22 (November 11 O.S.). Abigail Smith, the second of four children, born in Weymouth, Mass., to Reverend William Smith and Elizabeth Quincy Smith.

1748   King George's War ends.

1750   John attends Joseph Marsh's school in Braintree to prepare for college.

1751   September. Begins studies at Harvard College in Cambridge, Mass.

1755   French and Indian War (Seven Years' War) begins.

        July. Adams graduates from Harvard College with B.A.

        August. Begins teaching grammar school in Worcester, Mass.

November 18. Begins diary after experiencing earthquake in Braintree.

1756   August 21. Begins study of law under tutelage of James Putnam in Worcester.

1758   July. Attends Harvard commencement and receives M.A.

October. Returns from Worcester to live in Braintree.

November 6. Admitted to Suffolk County Bar, Boston; begins practice of law, Inferior Court of Common Pleas.

December. Loses first case as practicing lawyer.

1759   Meets Abigail Smith for the first time.

1760   Drafts essay on evils of licensed houses.

1761   British defeat French on Plains of Abraham.

February. Notes arguments in Superior Court of Judicature on writs of assistance.

May 25. Adams' father dies during influenza epidemic; as oldest son, John inherits Braintree property.

November. Admitted to practice in Superior Court of Judicature.

1762   Serves on town committees, travels Inferior and Superior Court of Judicature.

All New France passes into hands of Great Britain. George III ascends throne.

August. Adams admitted as barrister in Superior Court of Judicature.

October. Begins courtship correspondence with Abigail Smith.

1763   February 10. French and Indian War (Seven Years' War) ends; Treaty of Peace signed in Paris the following year.

James Otis delivers fiery address before the Superior Court of Massachusetts against use of Writs of Assistance by British customs officers. (Adams later saw this as the beginning of the American Revolution.)

June-July. Adams' first newspaper contributions, spoofing human nature and advocating a balance between monarch, aristocracy and democracy, appears in the Boston *Evening Post* and Boston *Gazette,* signed "Humphrey Ploughjogger."

October 7. King George signs Proclamation Act forbidding colonial expansion into Western Territories.

1764   April 5. British Parliament passes Revenue Act (Sugar Act) placing duties on all sugar imported into the colonies to support upkeep of British army in North America. James Otis makes a fiery speech that includes the line "No taxation without representation."

April-May. Adams inoculated for smallpox, in Boston.

Lord Grenville becomes English Prime Minister.

Treaty of Paris ending French and Indian War forces France to cede Canada and all her territory east of the Mississippi, except Isle d'Orleans, to Great Britain.

August 25. John Adams and Abigail Smith wed in her father's house in Weymouth.

1765   January. Joins lawyers' club in Boston to study legal history and theory.

March 22. British Parliament passes Stamp Act, first direct tax on colonies. Adams elected surveyor of highways in Braintree.

June. Travels eastern court of circuit to Maine for the first time.

July 14. Daughter Abigail (Nabby) born.

August-October. Adams publishes *Dissertation on the Canon and Feudal Law* in installments in Boston *Gazette.*

July. Lord Rockingham succeeds Grenville as British Prime Minister. Stamp Act, requiring stamps on newspapers, legal papers, pamphlets, playing cards, etc., becomes law

August. Boston experiences increasing violence as a result of Stamp Act. Adams writes, anonymously, that "liberty must at all hazards be supported."

September-October. Adams composes Braintree Instructions denouncing Stamp Act. Colonies meet in New York at request of Massachusetts. Stamp Act Congress, as it is called, protests to the King and Parliament.

December. Adams named counsel for Boston to plead for reopening of courts.

1766　January. Adams publishes "Clarendon" letters on British constitution and American rights in *Boston Gazette* .

March 5. Adams elected a selectman of Braintree.

March 19. News of repeal of Stamp Act reaches Boston.

June-July. British Parliament passes Townshend Revenue Acts imposing taxes on sale of glass, lead, paper, tea, and painters' colors.

July. Adams becomes active in improvement of professional practice of law through Suffolk bar association. Elected selectman in Braintree.

1767　July 11. Son John Quincy born.

October 28. Town meeting called in Boston to protest Townshend Acts.

1768　March. Adams declines to stand for Braintree selectman.

April. Moves family to Brattle Square in Boston.

June. Custom officers seize Hancock's sloop, *Liberty*.
Adams writes instructions for Boston representatives to
General Court protesting seizure.

October 1. Britain sends 4,000 troops to Boston to quell
protests against taxation.

December 28. Second daughter, Susanna born (dies
February 4, 1770).

Adams successfully defends John Hancock in admiralty
court against charges of smuggling in connection with
sloop *Liberty*.

1769   Spring. Adams moves family to Cold (Cole) Lane, Boston.
May. Writes instructions for Boston representatives to
General Court protesting presence of British troops and the
killing of Lt. Panton of British Navy.

May-June. Successfully defends Michael Corbet and
three other sailors in admiralty court against charge of killing Lt. Panton.

August. Takes on two law clerks (Austin and Tudor) for his
Boston law office.

September. Hired by James Otis as co-counsel following
Robinson affray (case concluded in Otis' favor, July 1771).

1770   January. Begins serving as clerk of Suffolk bar association.

March 5. Boston Massacre. Three persons killed, two
mortally wounded, six injured by British soldiers. Adams
agrees to defend Capt. Preston and men on charge of
murder.

May 29. Second son, Charles Francis, born.

June. Adams elected representative of Boston to General
Court (serving to April 1771).

October-November. Successfully defends Preston and soldiers in "Boston Massacre" trials.

Moves during year to another house in Boston, on Brattle Square.

1771   April. Moves back to Braintree. Strain of public life affects his health.

June. Travels to Connecticut to take mineral waters at Stafford Springs for health.

1772   Spring. Writes and presumably delivers patriotic oration in Braintree at request of town.

Committees of Correspondence organized in Massachusetts under Samuel Adams and Joseph Warren, followed by similar committees throughout the colonies.

September 15. Third son, Thomas Boylston, born.

November. Moves to Queen Street (later Court Street) in Boston, maintains law office there until outbreak of hostilities.

December. Successfully defends Ansell Nickerson in admiralty court against charges of murder; case concluded in July-August 1773.

1773   January-February. Publishes articles in Boston *Gazette* answering William Brattle and opposing crown salaries to Superior Court judges.

May. Elected by House a member of the Council but election is negatived by Governor Hutchinson.

December 16. Boston Tea Party.

1774   February. Buys father's homestead (later known as the John Adams Birthplace) from brother Peter Boylston.

March. Furnishes legal authorities for impeachment proceedings against Chief Justice Peter Oliver. Drafts report for General Court on Massachusetts' northern and western territorial claims.

May. Elected by House a member of Council but is negatived by Gage.

May-June. Coercive (Intolerable) Acts enacted in response to Boston Tea Party.

June. Chosen a delegate to First Continental Congress. Moves family to Braintree.

August 10. Sets off for Philadelphia with Massachusetts delegates to Continental Congress.

September-October. Congress, assembled in Philadelphia, protests British treatment of American colonies in Declaration of Rights and Grievances.

October-November. Returns from Philadelphia to Braintree.

November-December. Attends first Provincial Congress in Cambridge.

December. Reelected to Continental Congress.

1775 January 5. Adams publishes first *Novanglus* letters in Boston *Gazette* defending colonies against Tory view.

March. Elected a selectman of Braintree.

April 18. Eight hundred British troops leave Boston at night to seize a stockpile of patriot munitions stored at Concord.

April 19. Battles at Lexington and Concord begin American War of Independence.

Second Continental Congress meets in Philadelphia. Adams chosen delegate from Massachusetts.

April-May. Adams travels from Braintree to Philadelphia to attend Second Continental Congress, May-June.

June 15. Adams nominates George Washington to be Commander of Continental Army.

June 16. Washington accepts commission.

June 17. Battle of Bunker Hill (Breed's Hill).

July 3. Washington assumes command of 16,000 American militia outside Boston.

July 8. Second Continental Congress submits Olive Branch Petition to King George.

August. Adams returns to Braintree, attends Massachusetts Council in Watertown, is reelected to Congress.

September-December. Attends Continental Congress. Helps pass measures establishing Navy. Writes *The Regulation of the Navy of the United Colonies of America.*

October 1. Abigail's mother dies of dysentery epidemic. Disease also kills John's brother , Elihu. Adams appointed Chief Justice of Superior Court of Massachusetts in October. Accepts but never sits. Resigns in 1777.

December. Obtains leave from Congress to return to Braintree. Attends Massachusetts Council, visits army headquarters in Cambridge, reelected to Continental Congress.

December 31. Benedict Arnold, leading American troops, suffers disastrous defeat in attempt to take Quebec.

1776   January 9. *Common Sense*, pamphlet by Thomas Paine that stirs American people to patriotic fervor, published.

February-October. Adams attends Continental Congress in Philadelphia.

March 16. British troops evacuate Boston, ending 11-month siege.

March-April. Adams writes *Thoughts on Government.*

May. Advocates establishment of new state governments, writes preamble to resolution recommending such action.

June 7. Richard Henry Lee of Virginia presents resolution to Congress declaring that "these United Colonies are, and of right ought to be, free and independent states." Adams seconds the resolution.

June 12. Congress appoints committee to prepare plan of treaties to be proposed to foreign powers. Adams appointed president of newly formed Continental Board of War and Ordinance. Appointed to committee to draft declaration of independence.

June-September. Drafts "Plan of Treaties" and instructions to first American Commissioners to France.

July 4. Congress adopts Declaration of Independence.

September 15. British occupy New York City. Adams travels to Staten Island the next day with Benjamin Franklin and Edward Rutledge to confer with British Admiral Lord Howe.

November 21. Washington and remnants of Continental Army begin retreat southward across New Jersey.

November-December. Adams returns to Braintree, attends Provincial Congress as member from Braintree.

December. Reelected to Continental Congress.

December 8. Last of Washington's troops cross the Delaware as British troops appear on other side.

December 24. Washington wins decisive victory over Hessians at Trenton.

1777   January 3. Washington defeats three regiments of British troops marching to aid Cornwallis. Adams travels from Braintree to attend Continental Congress.

February 1. Philadelphia threatened by British, Congress removes to Baltimore.

Washington decisively defeated at Brandywine Creek.

March-September. Adams attends Continental Congress. Presides over Board of War and Ordinance.

June 14. Congress passes Flag Resolution for design of national flag that shall include 13 white stars in a blue field, and 13 alternating red and white strips. Betsy Ross selected to make first flag.

July 11. Third daughter, Elizabeth, stillborn.

September 26. British capture Philadelphia. Congress removes to York.

October 17. General Burgoyne surrenders army of nearly 6,000 British troops at Saratoga.

November 15. Second Continental Congress adopts Articles of Confederation. Adams obtains leave from Congress. Returns to Braintree, resumes law practice. Elected commissioner to France to negotiate a treaty of alliance, with Franklin and Arthur Lee, replacing Silas Deane.

1778　February 13. Adams leaves for France with son John Quincy to join Franklin and Lee as ministers plenipotentiary. French-American alliance signed February 6 while he is still at sea.

April. Adams moves in with Franklin in Hôtel de Valentinois in Passy.

May 8. Attended by Franklin and Lee, Adams presented to Court of Louis XVI at Versailles.

June. Great Britain attacks French ships at sea.

September. Franklin named sole minister plenipotentiary to France.

1779　February 11. News of Franklin's appointment at Paris.

March 8. Adams and son John Quincy leave Paris to return home. Delays at Nantes and Lorient keep them from sailing. Meets with John Paul Jones.

June 17. Sails from L'Orient for home in French frigate, *La Sensible*.

August 2. Adams and son reach Boston, return home to Braintree.

August 30. At a dinner in Boston, Adams proposes establishing American Academy of Arts and Sciences (it is established one year later).

August-November. Adams chosen to represent Braintree at Massachusetts Constitutional Convention. Is principal drafter of constitution submitted to voters.

October. News reaches Adams that on Sept. 27 Congress named him minister plenipotentiary to negotiate treaties of peace and commerce with Great Britain.

November 15. Sets sail once again for Europe on *La Sensible*, taking two sons with him this time, John Quincy and Charles Francis.

December 8. *La Sensible* springs leak, puts into port at Ferral, Spain. Impatient to be in Paris, Adams makes way across northern Spain to France by mule train.

1780   February 9. Adams arrives in Paris, settles into Hotel de Valois.

April 19-July 14. Composes *A Translation of the Memorial to the Sovereigns of Europe* (published in Amsterdam in November, and London in January, 1781).

May 12. America suffers worst defeat of war in Charleston, South Carolina. Almost 6,000 Americans surrender.

June 20. Congress commissions Adams to seek loans in The Netherlands.July. Writes articles published as "Letters from a Distinguished American" in London, 1782.

July 27-August 10. Travels to Amsterdam to establish relations with bankers and government officials who might be instrumental in obtaining loans.

October 4-27. Writes 26 letters to Hendrik Calkoen explaining origin, progress, and nature of American Revolution to Dutch.

October 25. Massachusetts adopts constitution proposed by Adams in convention, submits it to voters.

December 29. Commissioned by Congress to negotiate loans and treaties of commerce with The Netherlands.

1781　January 11. John Quincy and Charles Francis enrolled at University of Leyden.

March-May. Drafts and prints a memo urging Dutch to recognize America. Submits it to Estates General on April 19 and subsequently publishes it in newspapers.

June. Elected by Congress as first of five commissioners (along with Franklin, Jay, Laurens, and Jefferson) to negotiate treaty of peace with Great Britain.

July 7-August 27. John Quincy accompanies Francis Dana to St. Petersburg as his secretary and interpreter.

August-October. Adams seriously ill with fever in Amsterdam.

August 12. Charles Francis leaves The Netherlands for home aboard the American *South Carolina*.

Articles of Confederation become effective when signed by delegates of last state. Congress of United States assembles.

Lord Cornwallis and troops surrender to American and French forces at Yorktown, in Virginia, effectively ending hostilities with Britain.

1782　April 19. Estates General of Dutch nation recognizes American independence and Adams as minister plenipotentiary to The Netherlands.

April 22. Adams given audience by the Prince of Orange, Stadholder Willem V.

May 12. Purchases and takes up residence at Hôtel des Etats-Unis, America's first legation in Europe.

June 11. Signs contract with syndicate of Amsterdam bankers for loan of five million guilders ($4,000,000).

October 8. Signs treaty of amity and commerce with The Netherlands.

October. Travels from The Hague to Paris to join peace commission.

November 30. Adams, Franklin, and John Jay sign preliminary peace treaty between the United States and Great Britain in Paris.

1783   January 21. Formal preliminary peace treaty signed.

September 3. Adams one of signatures to definitive peace treaty between United States and Great Britain.

September-October. Adams falls ill for second time.

October 20. Ill, Adams sets out from Paris for London and the waters of Bath to recover health.

December 22. Washington resigns commission as commander-in-chief.

1784   January. Adams travels from Bath to Amsterdam under the most severe conditions of weather and terrain to renegotiate loans.

March 9. Adams concludes second Dutch loan in Amsterdam to save American credit.May-June. Congress elects Adams, Franklin, and Jefferson commissioners to negotiate treaties of amity and commerce with European and North African nations.

June 20. Abigail and Nabby sail from Boston for England.

July 21. Abigail and Nabby arrive in London.

July 30. John Quincy joins mother and sister in London.

John arrives week later.

August. Adams family leases manion at Auteuil near Paris.

1785   February 24. Adams named first United States minister to Great Britain. Jefferson joins Franklin in Paris.

May 12. John Quincy leaves for America.

May. Adams, Abigail, and Nabby take up residence in London.

June 1. Adams presented to King George III.

June 23. Abigail and Nabby presented to King and Queen (Charlotte).

July 26. John, Abigail, and Nabby move into first American legation in London, a house on Grosvenor Square.

August 17. Son Charles admitted to Harvard.

1786   January 25. Adams signs treaty of peace and friendship with Morocco.

March 15. John Quincy enters Harvard as junior. Graduates following year.

March-April. Jefferson visits Adams in London to negotiate commercial treaties with Tripoli, Portugal, and Great Britain; he and Adams tour English gardens.

August 30. Son Thomas Boylston admitted to Harvard; graduates in 1790.

August-September. Abigail journeys to The Netherlands with John to exchange ratifications of treaty with Prussia.

September-October. Adams begins *A Defence of the Constitution of the United States* in three volumes, which he finishes in 1787. Shay's Rebellion. Federal Constitutional Convention, called by Congress, meets in Philadelphia. New constitution drafted and submitted to states.

1787 New Federal Constitution accepted by sufficient number of states, becomes effective.

1788 Adams and family return to America from Europe.

1789 March. George Washington elected President of the United States, Adams Vice-President.

April 21. Adams takes oath of office.

April 30. Washington inaugurated.

July. Adams' son Charles Francis begins study of law in office of Alexander Hamilton in New York; later transfers to office of John Laurance.

1790 April. Adams begins publication of series of articles called *Discourses on Davila* in *Gazette of the United States*, which continue until April 1791.

November. John and Abigail move to new U.S. capital, Philadelphia.

1791 May. Adams elected president of Academy of Arts and Sciences; serves until 1813. Washington issues proclamation of neutrality in war between French and British.

June 8-July 27. At father's urging, John Quincy publishes "Publicola" essays in *Columbia Centinel* attacking Thomas Paine's *Rights of Man* and criticizing Jefferson's support of Paine.

1792 February 22. North Parish of Braintree, which includes "Peacefield," incorporated into town of Quincy.

August. Charles Francis obtains certificate to practice law.

Jay's treaty with British concluded.

1793 February. Washington and Adams reelected.

December. Thomas Boylston admitted to the bar in Philadelphia.

1794   May 30. President Washington appoints John Quincy resident minister to The Netherlands.

September-October. John Quincy sails to England with his brother Thomas Boylston, whom he names his secretary.

November 6. John Quincy presents his credentials at The Hague.

1795   January 27 or 28. Caroline Amelia Smith daughter of Abigail Adams Smith, born in New York.

August 29. Charles Francis Adams marries Sarah Smith, sister of William Stephen Smith in New York.

1796   May 30. President Washington appoints John Quincy minister plenipotentiary to Portugal, but John Quincy never serves under this appointment.

August 8. Susanna Boylston Adams, daughter of Charles Francis Adams, born in New York.

September 19. President Washington's "Farewell Address" published in Philadelphia *American Daily Advertiser.*

December. Adams elected President of United States, Jefferson Vice-President.

1797   March 4. Adams inaugurated as second president of United States.

March 25. Adams issues call for Congress to reconvene.

May 15. Congress reconvenes to consider difficulties with France.

June 1. Adams appoints John Quincy minister plenipotentiary to Prussia.

July 10. After approving first peace mission to France and passing an Act Providing a Naval Armament, Congress dissolves itself. Gerry and Marshall leave for France.

July 19. Adams and Abigail leave for Quincy.

July 26. John Quincy marries Louisa Catherine Johnson in London.

October. Adams and Abigail leave for Philadelphia, spend month with Nabby in East Chester upon hearing of yellow fever outbreak in Philadelphia

November 23. Adams delivers pessimistic address to Congress, forestalling rumors that the members of his commission would not be received in Paris. News of Napoleon's victories suggests France will be war-like toward U.S.

1798 March-April. Adams declares state of quasi-war with France, publishes XYZ papers.

May-June. Adams proposes, Congress approves, creation of Department of Navy.

July. Adams signs Alien and Sedition Acts.

November 12. Adams leaves Quincy for Philadelphia; Abigail, still recovering from sickness, stays behind.

November24. Arrives in Philadelphia.

December 7. Delivers speech to Congress; leaves door open for peace.

1799 February. Adams appoints peace mission to France.

July 11. John Quincy signs treaty of amity and commerce with Prussia.

October. Adams appoints second peace mission to France.

1800 May. Adams dismisses Secretary of War James McHenry and Secretary of State Timothy Pickering for opposing his peace policy.

September. Hamilton publishes *Letter…concerning the Public Conduct and Character of John Adams, Esq.* attacking Adams and his administration.

October. Convention with France ends naval war and Franco-American alliance of 1798.

November 1. Adams first president to live in President's House in Washington; Abigail joins him in mid-month.

December 1. Son Charles Francis dies of alcoholism.

December. Adams defeated for reelection.

1801 January-February. Adams appoints John Marshall Chief Justice of United States.

February. Adams recalls John Quincy from Prussia.

March 4. Jefferson elected President, Aaron Burr Vice-President.

Adams retires to "Peacefield" home in Quincy.

1802 October 5. Begins autobiography (works on it until 1807).

1803 November. Breaks with Massachusetts Federalists over support of Louisiana Purchase (he supports it).

1807 July-August. Writes ten letters to Mercy Otis Warren criticizing her treatment of him in her *History of the Rise, Progress and Termination of the American Revolution*

1809 April. Adams begins series of letters of reminiscence that are published in the Boston *Patriot* (they continue until to May 1812).

June 27. President Madison appoints John Quincy minister plenipotentiary to Russia.

1812 Adams renews friendship with Jefferson, beginning correspondence that lasts until their deaths.

1817 March 5. President Monroe appoints John Quincy Secretary of State.

1818 October 28. Abigail Adams dies in Quincy.

1820   Adams attends Constitutional Convention of
        Massachusetts.

1825   February 9. John Quincy Adams chosen President of the
        United States by House of Representatives after close elec-
        tion ends in tie.

        March 4. John Quincy inaugurated.

1826   July 4. Adams dies at Quincy, the same day as Jefferson.

Bibliography

Adams, Henry. *History of the United States of America during the Administration of Thomas Jefferson.* New York: The Library of America, 1986.

Adams, John, ed. *A Defence of the Constitutions of Government of the United States of America.* New York: Akashic Books, 2004.

Adams, John, ed. George A. Peek, Jr. *The Political Writings of John Adam: Representative Selections.* Indianapolis: Bobbs-Merrill, 1954.

Adams, John and Rush, Benjamin, eds. John A Schutz and Douglas Adair. *The Spur of Fame: Dialogues of John Adams and Benjamin Rush, 1805-1813.* Indianapolis: Liberty Fund, 1966.

Adams, John Quincy and Adams, Charles Francis. *The Life of John Adams.* Vols. I-II. New York: Haskell House Publishers Ltd, 1968.

Akers, Charles W. *Abigail Adams: A Revolutionary American Woman.* New York: The Library of American Biography (Third Edition), Pearson/Longman, 2007.

Bailyn, Bernard, ed. *Debate on the Constitution.* Parts I-II. New York: Library of America, 1993.

Bernstein, R.B., ed. *The Wisdom of John and Abigail Adams.* New York: MetroBooks, 2002.

Bliven, Bruce, Jr. *The American Revolution.* New York: Random House, 1958.

Bliven, Bruce, Jr. *Battle for Manhattan.* Penguin Books, Baltimore, MD, 1964.

Bowen, Catherine Drinker. *John Adams and the American Revolution. Old Saybrook, Ct:* Konecky & Konecky, 1979.

Brookhiser, Richard. *America's First Dynasty: The Adamses, 1735-1918.* New York: The Free Press, 2002.

Butterfield, L.H., ed. *Diary and Autobiography of John Adams.* The Adams Papers. Vols. I-IV.Cambridge, MA: Harvard University Press, 1966.

Cappon, Lester J. ed. *The Adams-Jefferson Letters: The Complete Correspondence between Thomas Jefferson & Abigail & John Adams.* Chapel Hill, NC: University of South Carolina Press, 1987.

Chernow, Ron. *Alexander Hamilton.* New York Penguin Books, 2005

Countryman, Edward. *The American Revolution.* New York: Hill and Wang, 1985.

Diggins, John Patrick. *John Adams.* New York: Times Books, Holt, 2003.

Ellis, Joseph J. *His Excellency George Washington.* New York: Random House, 2004.

Ellis, Joseph J. *Founding Brothers: The Revolutionary Generation.* New York: Knopf, 2001.

Ellis, Joseph J. *Passionate Sage: The Character and Legacy of John Adams.* New York: W.W. Norton, 2001.

Ferling, John. *Adams vs. Jefferson: The Tumultuous Election of 1800.* Oxford University Press, 2004.

Ferling, John. *John Adams: A Life.* New York: Holt, 1992.

Ferling, John. *A Leap in the Dark: The Struggle to Create the American Republic.* New York: Oxford University Press, 2003.

Ferling, John. *Setting the World Ablaze: Washington, Adams, Jefferson and the American Revolution.* New York: Oxford University Press, 2002.

Franklin, Benjamin. *The Autobiography of Benjamin Franklin.* Mineola, NY: Dover, 1996.

Grafton, John ed. *The American Revolution: A Picture SourceBook.* New York: Dover, 1975.

Grafton, John, ed. *The Declaration of Independence and Other Great Documents of American History, 1775-1865.* Mineola, NY: Dover Publications, 2000.

Grafton, John and Daley, James, eds. *28 Great Inaugural Addresses from Washington to Reagan.* Mineola, NY: Dover, 2006.

Grant, James. *John Adams: Party of One.* New York: Farrar, Straus and Giroux, 2005.

Hitchens, Christopher. *Thomas Jefferson.* New York: HarperCollins, 2005.

Johnson, Paul. *George Washington: The Founding Father.* New York: HarperCollins, 2005.

Ketcham, Ralph, ed. *The Anti-Federalist Papers and the Constitutional Convention Debates and the Clashes and the Compromises that Gave Birth to Our Form of Government.* New York: Signet Classic, 2003.

McCullough, David. *John Adams.* New York: Simon & Schuster, 2001.

McCullough, David. *1776.* New York: Simon & Schuster, 2005.

McDowell, Bart. *The Revolutionary War.* Washington, DC: National Geographic Society, 1967.

Morgan, Edmund S. *Benjamin Franklin.* New Haven, CT: Yale University Press, 2002.

Morgan, Edmund S. *The Meaning of Independence: John Adams, George Washington, Thomas Jefferson.* New York: W.W. Norton, 1976.

Nagel, Paul C. *The Adams Women: Abigail and Louisa Adams, Their Sisters and Daughters.* Cambridge, MA: Harvard University Press, 1987.

Nagel, Paul C. *Descent from Glory: Four Generations of the John Adams Family.* Cambridge, MA: Harvard University Press, 1999

Paine, Thomas. *Collected Writings.* New York: Library of America, 1995.

Peterson, Merrill D., ed. *Thomas Jefferson, Writings: Autobiography, A Summary View of the Rights of British America, Notes on the State of Virginia, Public Papers, Addresses, Messages, and Replies, Miscellany, Letters.* New York: The Library of America, 1984.

Rhodehamel, John, ed. *The American Revolution: Writings from the War of Independence,* New York: The Library of America, 2001.

Roberts, Cokie. *Founding Mothers: The Women Who Raised Our Nation.* New York: William Morrow, 2004.

Schiff, Stacy. *A Great Improvisation: Franklin, France, and the Birth of America.* New York: Henry Holt, 2005.

Smith, Page. *John Adams.* Vols. I-II. Garden City, NY: Doubleday, 1962.

Stone, Irving. *Those Who Love: A Biographical Novel of Abigail and John Adams.* Garden City, NY: Doubleday, 1965.

Taylor, Robert J., ed. *Papers of John Adams.* Vols. III-IV. Belknap Press of Harvard University Press, 1983.

Taylor, Robert J., ed. *Papers of John Adams.* Vols. III-IV. Belknap Press of Harvard University Press, 1983.

Thompson, C. Bradley, ed. *The Revolutionary Writings of John Adams.* Indianapolis, Liberty Fund, 2000.

Vidal, Gore. *Inventing a Nation: Washington, Adams, Jefferson.* New Haven, CT: Yale University Press, 2003.

Weintraub, Stanley. *General Washington's Christmas Farewell: A Mount Vernon Homecoming, 1783.* New York: Free Press, 2003.

Wills, Garry. *Henry Adams and the Making of America.* New York: Houghton Mifflin, 2005.

Wills, Garry. *Negro President: Jefferson and the Slave Power.* New York: Houghton Mifflin, 2003.

Withey, Lynne. *Dearest Friend: A Life of Abigail Adams.* New York: Touchstone, 2001.

Wood, Gordon S. *The American Revolution: A History.* New York: The Modern Library, 2002.

Index

John Adams

Dorchester Heights 46
Duc de La Vauguyon 77
"Duke of Braintree" 103
  Midnight Judges 144
Duquesne 8
Dutch Reform Church 170
Dyer, Joseph 10

E

earthquake in Braintree 9
East Chester 120, 125, 134
East India Company 35
East River 54
El Ferrol 63
Ellsworth, Oliver 130, 131, 133
  attempt to elect President 136
  Chief Justice 144
England, 153
  declares war against French 11
  John Quincy 157
  John Quincy and Louisa 157
  Rights of Man, 123
English Channel 82
Essay concerning Human
  Understanding 7

F

Faneuil Hall 28, 29, 32, 33, 161
Farewell Address, GW 111, 169
Federalists 116
  Adams 130
  Adams expects support 111
  Adams' speech 118
  Adams toadying to French 117
  attack on Adams 139
  avoiding war 118
  Cabinet 135, 137
  cause Adams problems 136
  conflict with Republicans 106
  defeat in New York 136
  High Federalists 127
  Jay treaty 110
  losses in New York 140
  peace mission 147

pressure for war 126
speech of Adams 127
upset by Hamilton scandal 119
Field, Joseph 15
Flynt, Henry 5
Forrest, James 32
Fort Duquesne 168
Fort Henry 12
Fort McHenry 156
Fort Ticonderoga 56
Fort Washington 54
Fort William 12
Fox, Charles James 78
France 71, 116, 131, 133, 147
  Adams appointed minister to 70
  admiration for Franklin 101
  capacity for war removed 126
  commerce 155
  crisis 125
  deteriorating relations 116
  Genêt 108
  peace commission 119, 120
  stalemate 127
  treaties of alliance/commerce 58
Franklin, Benjamin 76, 79, 80
  Adams at Versailles 65
  Adams 65, 72, 79, 101, 152,
  character and religion 170
  commissioner to France 52
  Congress 51
  Declaration of Independence 50
  eminent scientist 6
  French National Assembly 101
  honorary titles 101
  ill with gout 79
  minister to France 57, 59, 72
  Oswald 78
  Paris 59
  peace feelers 78
  sole minister plenipotentiary 60
  Vergennes 65, 66
  visits Lord Howe 53
Freeman's Farm, battles of 57
French and Indian War 11
French Directorate 125

206

About the Author

JOSEPH COWLEY was born on October 9, 1923. He graduated from Columbia University in 1947, interrupting his academic career to serve two and a half years with the army Air Force during World War II. The last few months of service were spent overseas as a bombardier with the Eighth Air Force, for which he was awarded a Bronze Star. He earned his M.A. from Columbia in 1948 and taught English at Cornell University before entering sales. Most of his career was spent writing on sales and management for The Research Institute of America. He took early retirement in 1982 to devote himself to his own writing.

He is the author of *The Chrysanthemum Garden* (published in hardcover by Simon & Schuster, 1982), *Home by Seven*, *Landscape With Figures*, *Dust Be My Destiny*, *The House on Huntington Hill*, all novels; and the plays *The Stargazers*, *Twin Bill*, and *A Jury of His Peers*; two collections of shorter fiction, *The Night Billy Was Born and Other Love Stories*, and *Do You Like It and Other Stories*; and, with Robert Weisselberg, *The Executive Strategist, An Armchair Guide to Scientific Decision-Making* (McGraw-Hill, 1969).

In 2006 he published a few of his favorite writings in *The Best of Joseph Cowley* as a tribute to his deceased wife. His articles have appeared in trade and science journals such as Jewelers Circular Keystone, *Our Army* and *Popular Mechanics*, and his short stories in *Prairie Schooner*, *New-Story*, *The Maryland Review*, *Ohio Short Fiction*, and other literary journals.

NOTE: Joseph Cowley has been listed in *Who's Who*, *International Who's Who of Writers and Authors*, *Who's Who in the World*, *Strathmore's Who's Who*, the *Cambridge Blue Book*, and other reference volumes. Among the few organizations he has been associated with are Mensa, Great Books, Authors Guild, and a 12-Step program.